The Healing Touch

Avril Wilson

The Healing Touch

The Healing Touch

For my wonderful girls Oshe, Serenity and Kalune
Their love, inspiration and comforting neighs inspired this book

Acknowledgements:
Writing this book has been like taking a long trek in the countryside on one of my horses; meeting rivers and obstacles on the way, fording streams and reaching heights. Alone it would not have been possible, but so many clever, knowledgeable and never-endingly helpful people came with me and offered me willingly advice, help and encouragement. I have learnt a great deal about horses and just as much about myself in writing this book.
My most grateful thanks therefore go to. Cast in order of appearance not importance.
Melanie Watson- instinctive horsemanship for her invaluable help right from the beginning with humour and insight Melanie guided me over the jumps and through the hoops of Running Wind's formative years; read my work, advised me and generally not only kept me company –but also kept me going. Melanie can –and does do all the things I have her do in the book.
Melanie Watson www.instictivehorsetraining.co.uk Main street, Cottingham, Yorkshire, HU16 5GT

David Chapman-Jones Tendon Works. I needed a way for Running Wind to be so badly injured that putting him down was a definite option especially if he was not insured, but also that he could feasibly recover from and perform again. David's brilliant input, insightful ideas and descriptions of real treatment were absolutely vital for the reality of this book. David's tendon treatment is real and does actually heal so many horses.

Dr David Chapman-Jones www.tendonology.com Burgess Hodson, Camburgh house,27 New Dover Road, Canterbury, Kent, CTI 3DN

Shane and Meredith Ransley came into my life when I was looking for help in training my 4 month old Arab foal Serenity I contacted Meredith looking for advice and help in this matter and found Quantum Savvy, I promptly signed up and joined and have since arranged two clinics here in France with Shane and Meredith. At the time Meredith gave me some golden advice. The input from Shane and Meredith has been instrumental in forming this part of the book. I wanted to show people that there is a better way to obtain a harmonious relationship with your horse than conventional methods portray and I believe that Natalie's Quantum Savvy journey sums this up perfectly. For the record everything Natalie does with her horse can be and is done by Quantum Savvy students round the world and I can ride my Arab mare Oshe bareback with just a string round her neck, in fact I have never ridden her using her a bit.

Shane and Meredith Ransley Quantum Savvy Natural Horsemanship Australia www.quantumsavvy.com

Monica Andreewitch and Tracy Edie both brilliant Quantum Savvy students have given me vital information and descriptions of their QS journey these I have added to my own emotions and unashamedly borrowed some for Natalie. The contact details for them and their groups are on the Quantum Savvy web site.

Monica and Melanie also gave me enormous help with the dressage parts of the book, excused me my ignorance and made Natalie's dressage journey possible.

Phillip Fuller funeral director of Southgate of Newmarket, was a great help giving me information he also asked Graham Locking racing minister at Newmarket if he would consent to his name being used.
Phillip Fuller www.southgateofnewmarket.co.uk
25 Duckers drive, Newmarket, Suffolk. E68 6AG

Pat Coleby's book was a great inspiration and provided me with a wealth of knowledge as Pat herself has done by letter, not only do I thank you again Pat but my healthy happy horses do too.
Pat Coleby Natural Horse Care www.acresud.com

Special thanks also to Ian Winfield and Vicki Thompson-Winfield for their permission to use Oldencraig as a venue in the book

Louise Shepherd for her insightful work reading my mind and working with me on the front cover. Cover design Louise Shepherd
louise@shepherdgraphics.co.uk

Also many thanks go to my two very hardworking volunteer editors Morven Boardman and Melanie Watson Any errors which remain are entirely due to negligence on my part.

Authors note

Although this book is essentially a work of fiction a great effort has been made to keep the facts as true and accurate as possible, any errors or deviations from facts are entirely my fault. While the story in this book and the main protagonists Natalie and the horse Running Wind are fictitious; many of the characters who appear in this book are real people. The actions I have them carry out in the book and the things I have them do are not only possible but are regularly practiced by these amazing, dedicated horse healers.

A donation from the proceeds of the sale of each book will go to The World Horse Welfare to help horses all round the world.

Web www.thehealingtouch.eu
Blog http://thehealingtouchbook.blogspet.com

The Healing Touch

'Life is full of beauty, notice it, notice the Bumble bee the small child and the smiling faces. Smell the rain and feel the wind. Live your life to the fullest potential and fight for your dreams.'
Ashley Smith

One white foot buy a horse, two white feet try a horse, three white feet look well about him, four white feet do without him.
Old Saying

Chapter 1   2003

The wind blew hard all day, and then picking up to nigh on gale force; by dawn it was so strong that when Malcolm Shand arrived, Bill was alerted only as the car headlights swung passed.

"About time," he muttered under his breath.

Malcolm looked over the door as the mare lay sweating on the straw, her flanks heaving as she strained, her neck stretched, and her head tossing in the straw.

"How long, Bill?" Malcolm asked.

"Nearly there now, ---look the forelegs and head are there."

"Can't you do something?" Malcolm insisted.

"Oh no, old Catcher knows her job. She hates interference." Bill replied confidently.

As they watched the mare gave one last heave and, with a sigh, pushed the foal into the world, her tangled mane slick against her wet neck.

Although he was nearly 60, Bill was into the stable in a flash to make sure the bag was ripped open and the foal could get air; he rubbed the shiny creature with a straw wisp as it bubbled to breathe. The wiry stock manger, with many years of experience behind him, looked on; he had seen hundreds of foals enter the world and nothing about this birth worried him. He reached out his hand to stroke the foal, bringing his head round so he could get a good look at him.

"A bay colt with a lightning blaze and a white sock, left hind." Bill said.

"He's fine, Bill?" Malcolm's voice was strained. He didn't like to think of how much the stud fees had cost him.

Bill knew what Malcolm meant; sometimes a foal was born deformed.

"Just perfect."

The first moments of a foal's life are magical.

Bill fed Catcher a hot mash feed and she stood slowly and carefully whickering to her new- born; at the sweet sound of his mother's voice the foal raised his head.

Both men watched as the colt tried to stand and control his out of proportion legs –for long minutes the little horse struggled with this most difficult first challenge in his life. Frequently he flopped over, but he was a determined little foal and after less than half an hour he was steady on his feet.

"Blue Maidens filly took two hours last week, "said Bill.

"You never know -- a real star winner." Malcolm replied laughing.

Despite the cold wind, the next day Bill led the mare and foal out into the paddock.Almost as soon as they were set free the colt set off, just running round his mother at first, then up and down the soft grass and over the wind. They could hear him squealing his pleasure at being able to run.

Bill turned to his boss.

"Well, what are you going to call him?"

3

The Healing Touch

"The wind blew when he was born, and it blows now as he runs, so if it passes Weatherby's --Running Wind he will be." Malcolm stated.

Whistling, Bill laid the feed bucket down; over the strong wind he could hear the drum beat of the hooves, long before he saw the colt. Two months old he seemed to be all spidery legs. He was running flat out, ears laid back. He was squealing as he ran.

"You had better be right –there's a lot at stake –is he really worth it? "
" I told you –I was there-- I saw him born and he was up in less than half an hour running like a pro the very next day –stake my life on it –he's the one. "Bill protested defensively.

"Well, you'll be back looking for another job again if he doesn't." John spat at him.Scowling Bill realized that he still had a lot of compromising and sacrificing to do to be with this horse. Never in his whole life of handling these majestic creatures had Bill even felt close to what he felt for Running Wind. He was also sure that in the wrong hands his young horse could go seriously wrong.

When Malcolm had announced it was time he was sold Bill had been devastated. Although he had known this was the colt's fate all along it now came hard to him.

He realised that the only way to stay with his 'boy'was to move to a training yard and hope to persuade the trainer to buy this colt.

"Lot Number 205 a Bay colt out of ----Jet Stream -- by Catcher in the Rye, set to make 16.2 a possible future high stakes winner." The auctioneer's loud, but disembodied voice rang out.

As the bell rang a young man entered the ring being towed by a sleek but powerful yearling colt that, as they passed the stand where Bill and John stood, was dancing on his hind legs and squealing as he did so.

"Oh, God, not this one." John remonstrated Bill.

"Yes, but wait until you see him really move. "

As the arena quietened the colt began to steady at last. He was strutting his stuff, walking out well with great extension and trotting alongside his handler.

"His movement is too high --it's a race horse I am buying, not a bloody ballerina!"

Bill was about to comment when the colt suddenly reared again and pulled free from his handler. He stood on the end of his rope tearing it free from the halter–he then sped round the arena for three laps and as the handler caught up with him, he swung his rear at him and gave him a double barrelled kick sending the poor man flying; squealing and bucking he set off even faster as three men now tried to corner him. Bill fought his impulse to go down and help, he knew Running Wind would come to him, but then Malcolm might find out that Bill was there with John Stride and work out why he had left his job of 20 years. He could hardly watch as holding ropes the men closed in slowly on the colt. Eventually winded and lathered with sweat the recalcitrant colt was caught –John was impressed with his speed –if not his behaviour.

"He's done us a favour. "Bill said sotto voce to John. "His price will go down." But he was wrong. The speed the colt had shown round the arena meant that other eyes were now upon him.

The hammer went up – bidding had started and quickly shot up – John was not prepared to go higher than £ 35,000 and when the bidding slowed the colt was finally bought for £ 42, 750.

Bill was devastated--- he had given up his job and now his colt had gone else where. He resolved to find out if he could possibly get a job in the yard his horse was going to.

"Right, Bill Harding --you say you are looking for a groom's job – you certainly seem old enough to have the experience –but at your age can you still handle race horses?" Trainer Bert Smythe had already decided to bring out his new and very difficult to handle colt; Running Wind, to test him – if he could work with this horse –he would get the job as two of his current grooms were quite frankly afraid of him and he had badly kicked Stuart the previous day.

As they walked into the yard the horses stuck their heads out to see who was there – suddenly from his box Running Wind let out a huge squeal – he had seen and recognised Bill. Bill decided to play this one straight and told Bert. "I was there at his foaling. He knows me." Bill went up to his horse that was nickering like a foal. As Bill came close Running Wind put his head onto Bill's chest and let out a huge sigh.
Bert was impressed." Lead him out, groom him and pick up his feet then lead him to the paddock. "
Slowly and calmly Bill entered Running Winds box and the horse dropped his head for the man to put on his head collar. Bert watched in amazement as this highly strung, difficult and often violent horse emerged from his stable like a docile puppy.
Bill kept the lead rope long and loose as he knew that most of Running Winds problems stemmed from insecurity and claustrophobia. Gently he groomed him all over – picked up his feet with no problems – after all it had been Bill who taught Running Wind to lift his feet and as he finished one the horse obligingly offered the next unasked. As Bill walked the colt to the turn out paddock Bert had made up his mind. "You can start tomorrow – your main responsibility is this colt – maybe now we can do some proper training with him. You have Siren in the next box as well." Bill was elated and relieved. He was back with his boy. Knowing that this would be the last great horse in his life he had decided to dedicate all his energy to this

horse. *He has the talent if we can find the right way to control him,* Bill thought to himself.

"Watch now, Colum, he's leery with this wind." Bill thrust the young Jockey into the saddle easily.

The colt set off bucking up the yard and Colum set his right rein hard over to try to steady him, Running Wind knew the drill now; a walk up to the downs then a brisk trot-- followed by a gallop over the top, but Running Wind wanted to gallop now!!

Three year old Drencher, already a race winner, came up alongside the colt and he just blew. The two set off.

Bert high on the downs was looking through his binoculars.

"What the blazes?"

He watched the two specs as they appeared on the horizon until he could identify the horses. Amazed he saw the two colts; Drencher, the three year old seasoned horse; a winner of several races and Running Wind the untried two year old, Drencher should have been several lengths ahead but as they came near to Bert they were neck and neck. As they drew level Running Wind passed Drencher easily. Bert could still hear the sound of his squealing echoing in his ears even hours later.

"It should not have happened – but what a horse!" he muttered to himself.

The sun was just appearing on the horizon giving an orange slanting light on the stables. A blackbird started his early morning serenade as Bill was tacking up. It was one of those rare mornings of complete calm, where every sound seemed amplified. The house door crashed as Bert came out; the ferocity of the crash telling Bill his boss was already in a bad mood.

He stood silently waiting to see who Bert would put up on Running Wind – whoever it was; it would not be a popular move with them.

"Joe Deakin can ride him." Bert announced.

"He told us last week he would not ride him again," Bill reminded his boss.

"Damn these young jockeys. It is not up to him – well, put that new lad, Steve, up."

"I doubt as he has the experience," Bill ventured.

"Damn you all – up he goes and he'd better stay there if he wants to have a job tomorrow." With that Bert strode off to drive his Discovery onto the downs.

Cursing, Bill went to find Steve, finding the rookie lad washing feed buckets by the tack room. Bill called over to him. "You're up on Running Wind in half an hour. "

Steve blanched and stuttered out "Nnnoo Mr Harding. I cccan`t ride imm."

Bill should have barked harshly at the lad but he knew his horse, and found pity. " Look lad I realise he's a bit of a handful, but if you are going to be a jockey you have to learn to ride all horses, I'll tell you one thing though, don't hang on his mouth --whatever else you do. "

Bill wished he was thirty years younger. He would have got up on Running Wind himself. He felt sure he could have controlled him.

Six horses set off towards the downs; they had to go across the main street and up a track through the woods before reaching the downs, while Bill followed with the quad bike behind.

All six horses lined up at the bottom of the rise and one by one they set off at the pace Bert wanted for their training. Second from last came Running Wind. "A good working canter till halfway then open him up to full race speed for the last couple of furlongs," Bill read off his exercise sheet.

As Steve set off gently at a good canter, Bill fervently hoped all would go well; this horse would never race if they could not train him to fitness.

Watching from afar as usual, Bert began to relax. His favourite moment of the day was seeing these beautiful creatures rise up the downs out of the mist, the plume of steam from their nostrils forming eerie clouds around them as they charged along, the heavy air covering the noise of their approach until they were very close indeed, when the thundering and pounding of their hooves, could be physically felt.

Running Wind passed Bert at full racing speed and carried on.

"Pull him up, lad! Bert shouted after him.

The horse carried on arcing round Bert and was now facing down the hill, still flat out.

"PULL HIM UP NOW!! " Bert bellowed, furious. Too much galloping at this stage of his training could undo the work so far.

White faced and hunched over the saddle Steve was completely out of control of this horse as he careered down the hill, Bill stepped out arms stretched at the bottom trying to turn him, but Running Wind crashed past.

Steve clung on, but it seemed the harder he pulled on and hung onto the reins, the faster Running Wind went. Despite the running martingale intended to keep his head down, the panicked horse had hold of the bit firmly and his head as high as he could get it.

Bill watched aghast as the boy and horse pounded through the woods heading for the main road. Running Wind was squealing as he ran.

Steve could only close his eyes; he knew the amount of traffic which would be on the road at this time of day. When they reached the road junction they should have crossed the road but the noise of the cars was too much for Running Wind and he veered right and set off down the pavement. They carried on parallel to the road, Steve forgetting Bill's words pulled even harder on the reins in a desperate effort to stop the horse. Already in uncontrolled flight mode, Running Wind started weaving and strayed onto the road then back; suddenly he swayed and Steve's leg crashed into a lamp post. Howling with pain Steve hauled again on the reins. Blood was running at the sides of the horse's mouth but no amount of pressure from the bit was going to affect him. The horse swayed again and this time he unseated Steve. The young lad lurched sideways off the horse, but his ankle caught in the stirrup his head bouncing off the tarmac inches from the steel clad hooves. The safety catch on the stirrup finally gave and Steve was left in a heap on the pavement.

Freed of the pressure on his mouth and Steve's body hunched up over his forehand Running Wind gradually slowed his pace. At the end of the road was another track to the woods, Running Wind took this track and as his adrenalin levels dropped he slowed to a walk, his head hanging low with the effort his sides heaving as he fought to catch his breath. By the time Bill drove the quad into the woods he was standing with his head nearly on the ground, completely blown. "Ach lad you won't be galloping the downs for a few days now will you. You will have to learn patience boy." Bill was relieved that neither horse nor lad had been seriously hurt though it would be a few weeks before Steve could ride again.

"Bloody hell, Bill. What do we have to do to train this horse?" Bert was beside himself with fury; his face always florid, was bright red. "Running Wind's training programme will have to be put back by two weeks and his first racing season starts next month."

Bill heard voices shouting, clattering hooves, and worrying crashes, as he approached the yard. Having put the two mares out in the paddocks with their foals, he was returning to take Running Wind to his field. He watched as John and two of the lads tried to get Springtide, a young mare, into the lorry. The mare turned her terrified eyes his way, as if appealing for help, and reared; striking out.

"Watch out!" Bert cried "The bitch is mad! She will kill some-one "He lashed the mare with his long whip and as he said this, the two lads closed in with a rope behind her. The mare reared one last time; then lurched into the lorry.

"Quick – up with the gate – we must leave. We are 1 hour late already – the stupid bitch."

Although Bill had not only witnessed, but also been party, to such treatment of horses before, he remained where he had stood long after the lorry had left the yard.

A loud neigh from the far side brought him back. Running Wind, his favourite horse, the best horse he had ever known, was calling to his buddy.

"Aye, lad, I'm coming to take you out, but I will never let you be treated like that." He spoke to the horse. Looking into the future Bill had seen the day only a few months hence, when Running Wind must himself be put into the lorry to travel to race. Only last week Bill had seen Bert choosing the races for his 'Star' horse.

It took Bill three whole days and nights to think of exactly how he could possibly get the very spirited horse into the lorry without him literally killing himself or someone. He knew that it must be secret, with no one else there, or it would not work. Late afternoons Bill decided were the best time as Bert had taken to going 'into town' -to the Bookies; Bill surmised, and the lads were usually crashed out asleep in the dorm, before their evening chores.

He knew it would not take long each day. *Little by little,* he told himself.

With the lorry ramp down – Bill led the horse near to the vehi-cle, he snorted when brought too close, Bill backed off and when Running Wind was calm, he laid down the feed bucket near the tailgate.

Over the next two weeks Bill slowly brought the horse closer until he could lay the bucket on the ramp – what Bill did not realise in this experiment in horsemanship was, that it was Running Wind 's trust in Bill which was growing – not his fear of the lorry diminishing. At 60 you have a lot more patience than at 6 or 16 –after 10 weeks Bill could walk into the lorry with the bucket, the horse at his shoulder, but, if Bill backed out of the lorry before he had finished eating, his horse would quickly back out with him.

"Next Tuesday Running Wind runs in a novice stakes at Bath." Bert was ecstatic. "At last we get to see our boy run!"

"Can we put the lorry here an hour early, and then I can walk him round the vehicle to get used to it?"

"Good idea, we do not want to set off late." Bert agreed.

What Bill really wanted was to be left alone to load the horse without any "help" or interference which could jeopardise his chances of quietly loading Running Wind.

Fortunately for Bill, just as the lorry was positioned in the yard Bert received an important phone call and returned to his office.

As soon as the tailgate was down, Bill took his bucket of grain and opened the stable door. He did not put even a head collar on the horse talking to him as he had done over the last few weeks; he calmly and gently led him into the lorry. Bill called quietly to Jim the driver to close the gate, but he remained with the horse. At the closing of the gate Running Wind started, but as Bill was there with him and calmly rubbing his neck, he remained still, and then he resumed eating his grain. Bill knew he had won and that the horse would travel without trouble to the race.

Bert was amazed that Running Wind was already in the lorry. He and Bill were also going along to see the star run for the first time. Somehow Bert had managed to persuade ex champion jockey Rob Steel to ride Running Wind in his maiden race – Bill imagined a lot of money had changed hands but he was delighted with the way Rob took to the young colt – he had ridden exercise on Running Wind this last week and the horse had never gone better. With Rob realising how important Bill was to the confidence of this equine, he insisted that Bill be beside him all the time until the run up to the start of the race. Rob also listened to Bill when he told him to avoid unnecessary pressure on the horse's mouth.

With Bill at his side leading him on a long rope Running Wind walked calmly round the parade ring. His coat shone in the spring sun like burnished copper and his black mane and tail were silky – he looked the picture of health and his pedigree had ensured quite steep odds. Bill surveyed the other 6 runners and guessed that there were two main contenders in this novice classified stakes ---River Bay, a big rangy colt, and Tide of Serenity, a grey filly who looked impressively fit as she danced and pranced round her groom. When Bill un hooked the rope and started to turn away Running Wind followed until Rob pulled him back round. As Bill looked back his horse was rearing and spinning. Bill was about to return and re hook his horse when Tide of Serenity came by at a gentle canter, Rob seized this chance and gave Running Wind a hefty kick sending him forwards out of his upwards spiral hot on the heels of the filly. "Whoa, man, this is not the race." Colum O 'Tool cried after him as horse and rider sped to the start. Rob knew he would be in trouble with Bert for his speed in the run up, but it would be worse if he could not even get the horse up to the start. Calling him by Bills nickname for him "Toady" and gently patting his neck Rob calmed the tense horse.

It had been arranged that a Monty Roberts loading blanket designed to help claustrophobic horses go into the stalls and a blind fold were to be used. Rob was pleased that they had been drawn midfield of the eight runners. Although he put up a bit of a struggle, getting Running Wind in was not as difficult as he had feared. Almost as soon as he was in and the gate behind him closed, the blindfold was removed and the gates in front opened. Bill watched from afar on the rails. The race had started and his boy was off, he was relived to see. There were two front runners pace-making, followed by five other horses well bunched and last was Running Wind – Rob had told Bill that he would keep him back at the start and let him settle then see if he could open the throttle about a third from the finish. Bert had given him no real instructions for the race and he was truly unsure how this horse would run – "Could he channel this power and speed?"

The noise from eight pounding animals was impressive as Rob, perched high on Running Winds withers, used the five horses in front to steady his horse knowing how touchy this claustrophobic horse was about his mouth being pulled. They swung round the tight bend and Rob was acutely aware of the horse, feeling his muscles thrust him forwards, hearing the pounding of the hooves, the air passing his head as the pace picked up again, and he thought, *they are going too fast – we'll never keep up this speed,* but was amazed how easily his mount was running. The ground going was good to hard giving a very fast pace.

He had to decide whether to swing right to the outside or left into the rails when he made his break –he had just decided on the freer running but longer route on the outside when the horse directly in front of him made a break right through the two front runners leaving a gap-- Rob did not hesitate and urged his boy after River Bay. The two horses surged through between the pace makers and accelerated again leaving the rest of the field behind –too late Colum tried to follow with Tide of Serenity. The filly made a brave running but was left in the wake of the two horses ahead of her. As they pulled away swinging in towards the rails Running Wind and River Bay were neck and neck; the crowds were cheering and Rob was elated. This was a much better position than he had dared hope for. His horse still felt powerful under him, his breathing loud but not laboured. Did he dare ask for more?-He lent even further forward his arms pumping and shouted "Go on, Toady, go." Running Wind's ears were flat back and as if in a direct reply he powered up from behind again. Rob felt as if he had changed gear in a racing car as they easily passed River Bay on his outside. Robs heart was pounding; he was amazed. "We're winning--- my God we're going to do it!" – Wryly he thought of Bill and how he had put a conservative £50 on each way not convinced of his boy winning first time out. Realising that he had not even had to raise his crop, Rob saw the finishing post so close he could nearly touch it. The cheering of the crowd was deafening as spent, the jockey sat back to try to ease the pace. Normally horses pull up not far beyond the post, but Running Wind carried on for many lengths until Rob finally managed to slow him to a trot and walk. Bill appeared as if from nowhere and a delighted Running Wind nickered at him as he threw a cooling string blanket over his boy. Bill was beyond happy. They had done it – his trust and faith in this superb horse vindicated. He was filled with such pride to see Running Wind in the Winners' enclosure. Bert was not happy – "Bloody hell, you nearly blew it racing up to the start – but a brilliant win! None the less! "He conceded…"That's it! You are a team. I want you up on him every time out." Rob patted Running Wind. *Not a bad afternoon he reflected, an important win and a definite ride on this talented horse in the future.*

Running Wind's win at Bath boosted the morale of the whole yard, and a second outing in a fortnight to Liverpool was planned. Bert had decided to go for a longer race at 7 furlongs which would be a challenge for most young horses, but Running Wind's ability to keep going after the race had impressed his trainer.

From the first moment when Bill had helped Rob onto his horse it was obvious that he was really on his toes. Even with Bill beside him Rob could hardly control this powerful athletic equine." If you can keep him steady and stay on, you should have a good chance. I doubt a lot of these youngsters are up to this length."

"Staying on will be the hardest part! " Rob laughed he had found to his cost last week how quickly Running Wind could spin and deposit his rider.

The strategy he had used at Bath worked for a second time as waiting for two horses to be making their way to the start Rob slotted in behind them.

Although this time just the Monty Roberts blanket was used, Running Wind went into the stalls without too much opposition.

Bill watched nervously as the last horse was loaded. Suddenly a horse reared up and crashed down onto the gate in front of it –designed to open to prevent injury in such an event the gate swung clear of the horse. Horrified Bill watched his boy as he set off down the track. Cursing Rob realised his chances of winning were slim as the horse wasted his energy; he used one rein to pull his mount round knowing he would simply rear or buck if he pulled too hard.

With Running Wind safely back in the stalls the gates opened and they were off. Running Wind in third place as the 9 horses galloped over the hard ground. Rob decided to just let his horse run and by the halfway mark they had gained on the second place horse, Molten Discovery. Rob could see Aiden Roach hitting his mount hard as he felt another horse approach. Digging in his heels he steered Running Wind away from the rails and passed the big chestnut gelding. Out in front the brown Walnut Grove was covering the ground with an easy long stride. Although they were slowly gaining on the front runner Rob knew they could not pass him before the post –one length behind they finished in second place. This time Rob leant right back and dropped his reins – his horse slowed immediately. Running Wind was blown completely. Now Rob's admiration for this delinquent horse now knew no bounds; a much longer race and a false start and still second place. This horse was going to one of the best rides of his career. Typically though, Bert did not share his admiration of the horse. "Wasted his energy again, bloody animal, he should have won." Rob imagined Bert had had a lot of money on his horse and was unable to look at things in the long term. As Bill appeared Bert harangued him as if the horse's well known character was all Bill's fault.

Later when Bert had gone off for a drink Rob reassured Bill that his faith in Running Wind was warranted. "He's a great horse. Wait and see. He will win again next time out."

Rob was right as Running Wind went on to win his next two races. One was a handicap race and due to his wins he was carrying quite a lot of weight – born in February, however, meant that he was actually 26 months old and therefore had a big advantage against the later June foaled horses. Nothing seemed to phase him once he was actually on the track. He knew what was required and was keen to win. As the odds on him increased,

Running Wind was himself becoming more domineering in the yard– only Bill of all the men could really control this horse. Bert did not care; he was winning more money through this horse than any he had ever had in his yard before.

Late September Rob drove into the yard for a briefing with Bert. Running Wind was to race the next day at Kempton Bert's Land Rover Discovery was not in its usual place. Rob climbed out of his car looking for Bill but there was no sign of either man. Increasingly frantic he ran to Bert's house, the office was on the ground floor, his chair was on its back on the floor and the telephone receiver had not been replaced in its cradle, signs of a hurried departure. Rob wondered what was going on. The evening before a race Bill was always with his boy, brushing and talking to him. Rob's heart sank; a shudder of premonition ran through him. Running in from the yard, one of the lads shouted, "Bert's gone to the hospital in Newmarket. There's been a crash! Bill's van has been hit by a lorry on the ring road. He's been badly hurt, his legs have been crushed they had to cut him out." Rob walked out again and stood staring at the horses' heads all out watching, waiting for their evening feed; his eyes rested on Running Wind for a long time. Bert would not withdraw a horse from a race just because his groom was hurt.

There is something about the outside of a horse that is good for the inside of a man.
Winston Churchill

Chapter 2

Walking as fast as he could through the ward Rob caught sight of Bill, last of four men on the left with four more facing them. Bill looked as if he were trying to get out of the bed despite his leg being attached to a sling above him.

"Steady up, Bill, you'll break your other leg." Rob laughed sitting down in the plastic chair to the side of the bed. He threw a copy of the Racing Post and a bar of chocolate on the bed, but Bill ignored them. Leaning forward he demanded loudly, "How's my boy? " --"Tell me he's OK. " Bill was nearly shouting and many of the occupants of the other beds were looking over.

Rob smiled wryly as he hurried to reassure Bill. "He's fine, fit as a fiddle physically – acting very unstable mentally though." He added. "Steve has a broken ankle and Bert cracked ribs. They never even got him near the lorry; after nearly two hours they took the filly Siren to the races on her own. Running Wind was in the big paddock and no one could get near him. Bert called me yesterday after the races and I went over this morning. Running Wind had been left out all night. I took a feed bucket and talked to him as you told me, calling him `Toady' – he snorted a bit but settled to his feed and let me catch him and lead him back into his stable."

Leaning towards Rob Bill whispered. "I have to get out of here, Rob. He'll kill someone. Then that'll be the end of my boy." His eyes were pleading in his thin and sallow face. Rob thought he looked years older than before the accident.

"You can hardly walk around attached to that pulley contraption"; Rob reasoned. "How long do the doctors say till you can walk?"

"At least six more weeks, maybe longer, at my age – what will happen to my boy?"

"Fortunately there are no more races planned for him for a couple of weeks and I will continue to ride exercise on him. Not one of the lads will get up on him again. There has been a mutiny and Bert holding his cracked ribs had to give in."

Bill looked depressed. "This is the worst thing which could have happened. Although he is a difficult horse his winnings were so high Bert was able to forgive him so much –but if he doesn't race again soon Bert will cut his losses. He needs to keep his lads, but most of them are such babies when it comes to difficult horses."

Rob could think of no words of comfort. He knew only too well how it worked in training stables. The lads were crucial to the smooth running of the place and if they refused to work with a particular horse it would simply be sold on to the highest bidder.

Rob had hardly turned off the engine of his Jaguar when Bert wrenched open the door. "Thank god you are here!" He cried. "That mad bloody horse is out again. Steve led him out to the paddock yesterday and there's been no way to catch him since." Bert was flushed and obviously very angry.

With falling spirits Rob saw that his hope that the horse was calming a bit was dashed. Running Wind had been easier to handle and ride this last week, but due to race commitments Rob had not been to the stables for two days. A horse that would not even come in for his feed and some warmth at this time of year was indeed a stressed horse.

His heart heavy the jockey walked towards the paddock. Bert, still ranting and raving in Rob's ears. The bay horse was at the far end of the large paddock.

As the men approached he raised his head his ears revolving as if listening in all directions at once. When they reached the gate Running Wind's head went even higher and his ears went flat back, he bared his teeth and pawed the ground. To Bert's amazement Rob did not however walk towards the horse. He stood very still at the gate, the head collar he had picked up from the ground by the gate unhidden in his hand. "Go and get a bucket of feed," he hissed at Bert.

He then started walking in the field not towards the horse but away from him. When he was as far away as he could get from the horse he sat down.

Horse and man were very still just looking at each other; with finally a huge sigh Running Wind dropped his head. Bert appeared with one of the lads carrying a feed bucket. "Lay it down out side and leave me alone with him," Rob said calmly. When neither man moved he repeated his order with more determination in his voice and added, "Or I will leave you to do it." Steve looked at his boss who nodded and the two retreated out of sight. Rob crawled over to the fence and retrieved the bucket still on his knees. He returned to the same spot he had been at before. The horse snorted but did not move. Rob did not look at the horse but gently rattled the bucket. Eventually after what seemed like several hours but was probably not even one hour Running Wind walked over and sniffed at the bucket. Rob willed his body to be completely still until the horse had started eating. Calling the horse `Toady' he remained bent over and started caressing his flanks. After a few minutes Rob stood up and slowly with no fuss put the head collar on .When he had finished the feed Running Wind allowed Rob to lead him back to his stable.

"That's it!" Bert said as they looked at the big Bay animal. "I have had enough of this beast. Jimmy Shanks has bought him. He'll pick him up tomorrow. "

"Not Shanks—he's a brute "–Rob replied aghast!

"Birds of a feather can make their bed together, then" Bert was belligerent and obviously determined. "Thinks he can tame him and make a packet –Ha –we'll see. This is the most difficult horse I have ever had in this yard and his disruptive influence has upset even the gentlest of the mares. I won't have him here any longer –Shanks has offered me £22,000 for him nearly half of what I paid."

"But what about Bill? He will be back in a few weeks –his boy will be fine then."

"What about Bill! –if you think I am keeping a dangerous horse in my yard till some old has been lad comes back in a couple of months, then think again!"

Rob was visibly upset. He had really enjoyed riding this horse which had been so good for his career, and just what would he say to poor Bill?

Rob put a lot of his spare time into finding Running Wind and in fact followed his trail to two yards. Apparently Shanks only had him for three months. He seemed very annoyed about the whole affair when Rob went to see him and not a little reluctant to give much information.

"So you never actually got him to a race? "

Shanks did not look Rob in the face as he answered, "Not as such."

"What do you mean?"

"Oh we got him to a race course alright, even got him to line up, and then he dumped Stuart Roberts at the start. He reared and then swung round, stamped on Stuart's foot and broke his ankle. I could swear he did it deliberately." Shanks shook his head. "Grahame Dixon is the best head lad I have ever had and he has always been able to handle the difficult horses. This horse is mad, totally crazy. Believe me, he will never race again."

"Where has he gone now?"

"I sold him on to Weeks – I was lucky to get £5,000 for him – worst deal I ever made in my life –I don't ever want to hear about that bloody horse ever again, so clear off."

"Weeks! That shifty, eyed gypsy –Oh God what next? I bet he won't keep him for long."

Rob parked his Jaguar next to a battered old Mercedes and a dirty looking mobile home. Behind were 4 wooden loose boxes but only one head looked out, a shaggy black and white one. Rob went up to the horse and put out his hand to stroke, it the horse flinched back as if it thought he would hit it. He saw a raw weal on its neck, a long stick with knotted bailing twine attached was propped by the door. Rob shuddered. A fat, bald man wearing a T-shirt that was full of holes with dirty stains down the front and low set even scruffier jeans under his huge belly, stood at the door of the mobile home.

"What de yer want?" he shouted at Rob.

"I'd like to ask you about a horse you bought from Shanks two months ago."

"None of yer business, "He turned and went back inside.

Rob walked up to the caravan a strong smell of chip grease and stale alcohol met him. He knocked on the door.

"Mr Weeks I would like to speak with you please. "

Silence.

Rob decided he did not have time for games. "It's worth £ 10" he held the tenner up to the window.

The door opened and the note was snatched from his hand.

"What `orse? "

"A bay race horse called Running Wind. "

"Ees not ere."

"Where is he now? "

"Took `im to the Shaddleford market an sold `im. "

"Who to?"

"None of yer business; ee were a rotten un, yon orse. "

"Did you drug him to sell him on?"

"Yer`ve ad yer "tanner's worth." Weeks simply turned his back on Rob showing a grubby bum slit above his jeans. He slammed the door of the caravan making it shake.

Depressed Rob realised he was unlikely to find a horse sold on drugged at a gypsy fair.

"So, Melanie, will you at least go and see him? " Desmond Wilks asked persuasively."He knew what her answer would be even before she uttered it. This was not the first time he had made such a request.

"Of course I will. I won't see a horse put down needlessly. What makes you think I can help him though?"

"Let's put it this way, Melanie Watson, I have never seen a horse you cannot handle yet! George Murphy bought this horse from Weeks at the Shaddleford market. That was about six months ago. Of course, he was calm at first and Weeks sent him on with a supply of er…cough medicine –It ran out at last and he bolted out with George's daughter Susan on board –he threw her into a wall and she has a broken wrist and collar bone. He was then sold on a month later to Arthur Black. I was called in by the RSPCA to look at several horses under Blacks not so tender care. I tell you Melanie I have never seen such treatment of horses in all my years. There were 20 horses in all; sadly I had to put three down as they were beyond help. Some of the others were not too bad and are being rehomed by the World Horse Welfare. A local rescue group have taken four; two geldings and a mare and foal that need a lot of treatment. But this horse is too much for them to handle."

"So he has been at this stable being badly treated for 5 months?"

"Yes it looks as if he has neither been out of the stable, nor fed much in all that time. At least the yard was once a good one and water is supplied automatically or we would have been taking away just corpses."

"Oh God!" Melanie's voice was thick with shock and anger.

"The RSPCA officer Brian Court took me aside. He reckoned that this horse was in too bad a mental state to be rescued. He recommended I put him down," The vet explained.

"Phew, and you think I can handle him? "

"I knew you'd take him Melanie. I told them you'd fetch him tomorrow."

Replacing the telephone receiver Melanie was in a reflective mood- another misunderstood horse on his way to the butcher's –well, thanks to Desmond he had a chance now.

Melanie was met by chaos when she arrived at the yard. The last of the horses were being loaded into a lorry by two RSPCA officers while a small pig faced man shouted at them.

"You can't take them. They're mine!" His little eyes were pale blue in a puffy pink face. He looked greedy and cruel, and stamped his foot in fury, but the two men ignored him. They had seen it all before.

Melanie parked her trailer next to the lorry and introduced herself to the officers. She looked across at the angry man, then over at the two officers.

"Don't worry about him. The horse you want is in this box. Call us if you need a hand but we will need to leave soon we have 6 horses in the lorry and I don't want them in there longer than necessary."

Melanie was led to the last box on a row of eight. She could already smell the rotten straw and old horse manure and acrid urine.

The awful stench that met Melanie as she approached the box was soon overpowered by the sight which met her eyes. At the back of the box a horse stood hock deep in manure, his back to the wall. The horse was seriously malnourished; his ribs showing and his hips jutting out. His coat was filthy with dung and his mane so tangled and matted it would probably have to be hogged. Melanie gasped. "I don't think he has been out of this box for weeks, if ever since he came here." The RSPCA man informed her. "No one could handle him. Joe here tried but we have too much with all the others to spend any time with him. Do you really think you can get him out of there?" He looked closely at this very attractive but slim young woman –he was trying not to be sceptical, but this was a crazy, mistreated horse. His own opinion had been that he should be destroyed. Without even answering, Melanie un-hooked the door to the box. Her heart thumping with anxiety and a touch of justified fear Melanie turned her attentions to the horse. His eyes were rolling, showing white and the muscle under his neck was rigid... throwing his head high. *This horse is ready to fight for his very survival; he has been so badly treated by a savage man, so I just have to get this horse out of here.* Speaking gently to the horse she entered the stable with the halter and lead in her hand in open view. Standing defensively at the back of the stable the horse watched her with flared nostrils and his ears flat back. Suddenly he came forward his teeth bared, ready to lunge and bite. Quickly Melanie reacted and using her long rope moved the horse sideways round the stable until she had her back to the wall and he was by the door facing her. They stood facing each other for a while then Melanie reached out her hand to the horse and very gently stroked his nose before he could react. She then moved him again and again round the stable. Each time he stopped and faced her she called him a good boy and stroked his nose. This confused the horse, who was anticipating more whipping and pain. She waited- every time she moved him- until he was focused on her. She wanted him to realise that she would not hurt him and that to be with her was a good and comfortable place to be. After 20 minutes, where Melanie remained calm and totally focused on the horse, finally she decided he was ready to be led. She approached him again and stroked his nose calling him a good boy. Gently putting on the halter and attaching the rope she simply opened the door and walked out of the stable. She was confident now to put a little pressure on the rope; The horse followed!.... At first hesitantly, obviously not sure of his feelings towards this human, but then more confidently as Melanie had shown him that with her was safety and he was too surprised to refuse. The two RSPCA officers looked on amazed as this slight woman emerged from the stable with the horse they had decided needed putting down.

"Please keep back!" Melanie had called to the men. "It will only upset him if you get too near. I can fill in any necessary forms later at my yard in Skidby."

They had finished loading and were moving towards her and the horse. At this Running Wind's head shot high again as he braced his legs. Melanie saw with respect for the horse, that he was preparing to defend himself again. Despite all that had happened to him in such a cruel and undignified way, this horse was not ready to give up. Melanie moved him round again and as soon as he was more relaxed and lowered his head, she rewarded him with a stroke on his nose. The RSPCA lorry left the yard and the pig face man turned on Melanie. He stepped towards her shouting that she was stealing his horse.

As he approached, the horse swung his hind quarters round and struck out behind. Although the kick missed him, Black jumped away alarmed and slunk off still grumbling.

Melanie just stood quiet with the horse telling him *"what a good boy he was and right now we are on our way mate –thank god for that!"* As her heart rate steadied she then walked the horse round her car and horse box, she had deliberately left the ramp down. As she moved the horse moved; when she stopped... the horse stopped. When she went forward or backwards... so must the horse. To the horse, who had already been looking at her in a different light, she was coming forward in his own language as a leader.

Having had a chance to look at the horse in better light, Melanie realised that this was no ordinary hack. Despite his emaciated appearance and louse ridden coat she saw real quality bone structure and a carriage and movement which spoke of excellent breeding. *He looks like a race horse but moves like a dressage horse, this is one special boy.* When she walked calmly into her horse box she did not look back. Even when she felt a slight tension on the rope she just continued in with great confidence. The horse followed her in and gave a huge sigh as she attached him. He seemed to be looking at her through different eyes.

It had taken her two hours on the phone, then the internet, to confirm the identity of the horse. The RSPCA had visited her with the necessary paperwork. Several of the rescued horses had been freeze marked and easily recognised. Only one set of papers for a thoroughbred were amongst the cache seized by the RSPCA. Using their digital chip reader the officer had confirmed that the micro-chip was for a horse named Running Wind. Research had come up with details of his breeding and his racing career. *He had been a very successful horse with; one would assume a great future. What on earth had happened to provoke such a rapid down wards spiral?*

Curling her feet under her and taking another sip from her glass of wine, Melanie read on. The records of every race Running Wind had run in spread all over the settee. Something struck her –she looked back to check –yes, she was right; in every race he ran in there was the same jockey on board! Although she knew that particularly with young horses the same jockey often rode a horse several times, but in every race? This must have meant that either the jockey or the trainer were making sure their time-tables coincided.

Rob Steel....Melanie knew the name, but had never met this particular jockey. Her work rehabilitating and helping troubled race horses meant she was well known on the race circuit –she picked up the phone and dialled a number......

Ten minutes later, after a lot of bantering small talk, she wrote a number down on one of the sheets before her.

Dialling a second time she thought about what she would say, but when a deep, interesting voice replied cheerfully she just rushed straight in. "Hi, you don't know me, but you may have heard of me. My name is Melanie Watson. I run a yard in Skidby, East Yorkshire and one of the things I do is to help troubled or difficult horses. I have just taken a horse into my yard which you rode in many races. His name is Running Wind. "As she said these last words she heard a sharp intake of breath.

"So he is still alive then. I thought he'd be dead by now! "

"I am sorry to say that I am his last chance. Desmond Wilks the Newmarket vet phoned me and told me he was due to be destroyed. I picked him up two days ago."

"You picked him up! –You mean you loaded him into a horse-box on your own?"

Melanie laughed at his shock "Yes, my head girl, Carlie, was too busy and I had to pick him up before the meat lorry got there!!"

Rob was seriously impressed and his interest was growing!– any woman who could load this horse on her own was worth talking to. "What can I do for you then Melanie?"

"I am looking for information on this horse, anything you can tell me about him…any information which will make my job of rehabilitating him easier. You rode him in many races –how was he to ride?"

"Well, I guess you would not have him with you if he was a calm easy horse, but from a jockey's point of view he was a superb ride. Once you got going in the race he wanted to win and he was a supreme athlete. I had some great wins on him."

"What was he like off the track or to load, in the stable, paddock, or to groom?" Melanie questioned.

"As long as Bill was with him – he was fine, very easy really – wouldn't have any of the other lads near him though." Rob paused then continued–"without Bill beside him he's a nightmare, bolshie, aggressive and vicious."

"Bill?"

"His constant groom since he was born, Bill Harding –this horse and he have an amazing bond. With Bill he is easy gentle and calm. The problems started when Bill was injured in a crash. When he went into hospital Running Wind went crazy. No one in the yard could control him. Bert quickly sold him on."

"Yes I know the story. "

"What happened to Bill then?"

"He was devastated when he heard that his boy had been sold on and Bert would not tell him who had bought him." Rob sounded reflective.

.

"I last saw Bill about 10 days ago. He did not look well although his leg is healing. He was grey and thin wanted me to help him find the horse. I don't think he has found a new job either."

"Do you know where I can find him? " Melanie requested.

When the bus turned into the market square Bill got to his feet and picked up his old rucksack. As he stepped awkwardly down the steps he saw the car a big green 4x4. An attractive woman, with long brown hair stood by the open door, her foot on the step.

Settling into the front passenger seat Bill asked "What is all this about, Ms Watson? All Rob said was for me to come here today. He said you wanted to see me and there might be a bit of work like."

Melanie smiled, "Wait and see. I have a surprise for you!"

The yard, when they reached it, was spotlessly clean; Bill was impressed. Several horses' heads appeared over their bottom doors as they parked.

"This way." Melanie led Bill towards a big field in which a handsome bay horse was cropping grass, his back towards them.

Bill stopped short. His hand went to his mouth; he dropped his rucksack and rushed limping towards the fence whistling as he ran, with Melanie running after him....

With a loud squeal the horse raised his head and swung round, already moving forwards, and galloped up to the fence where Bill was climbing up. Bill sat on the fence holding Running Wind's head. Melanie was delighted. She was glad that Bill who so obviously thought the world of this horse had not seen him in the state he was 4 months ago. It had taken all her skill and patience to bring this horse back to health. Although he was not completely back in condition, it helped that it was late spring and there was plenty of grass. Carlie, her head girl, had helped her to apply the insecticide and dress his many wounds. Fortunately there were no serious injuries and Desmond was happy to leave the treatment to Melanie. The biggest worry for Melanie had been how to get his very badly neglected hooves dressed.

The farrier had tried once but Running Wind would not stand and give his feet to this man. Now with time and perseverance his feet could be trimmed and the real work start.

Within a couple of days Melanie saw the wisdom of her tenacity in tracking down Bill; the horse was so much calmer and seemed so much happier. Yesterday the farrier had trimmed his feet which now looked a lot better; but Richard Cross had said it would take several more trims until all the cracks were gone. *Now we can get to see what he can do.*

Twilight sounds echoed round the yard. Starlings flocking before they roosted, and groups of up to fifty individuals swooping and soaring in such perfect unison that they looked like a shoal of fish. A very harassed looking Bill led a subdued Running Wind into the yard. Melanie turned to them, a quizzical expression on her face.

"Jumped into the orchard again didn't he?" Bill explained. Shaking her head Melanie looked flabbergasted. "That fence is 1 meter 20 high –and he jumps it just to get a few apples!"

"Apples always were his favourite. Now he knows how to get them there'll be no stopping him." Bill was trying not to laugh.

"Even so, not many horses will jump of their own free will- some do in great fear, others. Hmm- bring him to the indoor school first thing tomorrow. I have an idea."

Relieved that Melanie was not angry, Bill happily complied.

Running Wind snorted as they entered the dusty interior of the school. Bill led him straight in. Melanie was setting up jumps down the long side of the school and Carlie was making a barrier on the other side of the jumps... to create a jumping lane.

Bill closed the door and stood looking down the row of jumps. When he saw the last one, he knew immediately what Melanie had planned.

"Take off his halter and stand back with Carlie."

As she spoke Melanie took up a schooling whip. At first she just sent the horse gently round the school so that he could warm up his muscles and get used to the obstacles. Then she upped the speed and the pressure. Normally Carlie would stand at the top of the jumping lane to help prevent the horse from running out, but Melanie had been specific in her instructions. The horse was to run free and be able to choose to avoid the jumps if he wished to do so.

As he came round fast the first time Running Wind did balk at the jumps but as he ran passed the last one he gave a sudden jump into the air as if leaping an invisible jump! They all laughed at this and Running Wind squealed. The next time round he made a deliberate swerve and set off down the lane. The first jump was only a small cross pole and he seemed to just stride over it....but the next was a larger straight up right pole, about two feet from the ground. Although he took off well he dragged his hind legs and the pole dropped to the ground. The third jump, however, included a filler. It was a little higher and this time the horse soared over without so much as touching it. When he saw the last jump he seemed to hesitate then he carried on with his ears pricked and easily jumped the obstacle. It was a reproduction of a brush hurdle of the type used in jump racing.

Melanie lowered her whip expecting the horse to slow down and ultimately stop, but to their amazement he continued cantering round and went down the lane again squealing as he ran.

He cleared all four jumps and set off round the school with a squeal of delight! Not wishing him to go on Melanie signalled Bill to recall his horse. Running Wind performed a beautiful flying change of cantering legs as soon as he heard Bill's whistle. He wheeled round and stopped directly in front of the man....his sides heaving.

"Well Bill, what do you think of your horse now?"

Amazed and delighted Bill patted his boy "He really seemed to enjoy jumping those obstacles!"

"Exactly." Melanie's voice was full of enthusiasm. "You could really see his tremendous confidence and joy. He obviously wants to jump –you see, Bill, he is finally being allowed to express himself and is offering fabulous free movement- now we can truly see what is in his heart!"

Never one to hesitate once she had a direction, Melanie started work in the school with Running Wind the very next day. With Bill standing close by she worked him over cavaletti poles from the ground whilst long reining him.   As long as Bill was there Melanie could easily really work with this horse. They started with Bill leading Running Wind round first with just the saddle on; then Melanie got on gently. Very quickly, as soon as Melanie was confident in the trust of this horse, they progressed to her riding round with Bill in the centre of the school.

Bill, so pleased to yet again watch his boy working, thought that a silken thread of life must run between them both....Running Wind was his destiny!

Although her horse was only 4 years old Melanie found that he was supple and tireless. It seemed to her that he realised that she had saved him from the hellhole stables where he had been so badly treated. He tried so hard for her with anything she asked him to do or try.

"Ok, Bill, lets see what he is made of today!"

Over the last few months the horse had been jumping better and better. Melanie had decided to try him out over a few of her cross country jumps. Bill walked ahead off them to the bank, where a set of three big steps made a flowing triple jump.

"I`ll try it going up first," she said laughing." You go and stand at the top so he will want to go up."

Puffing as he climbed, dragging his leg a little, Bill stopped almost at the crest of the bank and stood a slight bit off to the left.....just in case Running Wind hesitated or drifted.

Melanie swung the horse round in a large arc to give him a good look at the jump and to give him the momentum he needed. Running Wind pricked his ears as he cantered up to the bank. Bill`s instructions had been to call him up if he hesitated in any way. Meeting the bottom of the bank in a good bouncy stride Melanie knew instinctively that no encouragement was needed. Running Wind attacked the bank with courage, enthusiasm and not a small amount of style. Reaching the top Melanie was so impressed; she simply turned her mount around and set him for the descent. Again Running Wind took the steps, which were each about 1 meter 20cms high easily and more importantly safely. When they reached the bottom Melanie gave a great whoop of joy! During the next few days she took the horse over ditches, fallen logs, brush fences and into and across the stream.

"Well Bill. What do you say?" Grinning hugely, Melanie encouraged a stunned looking Bill to reply.

"Hunting?"

"Yeah let`s take him hunting! How about a drag hunt? Then we can see what he can really do! Go on...are you up for this? I know of a good hunting pony. You can come with me and keep an eye on your boy!"

Bill was seriously tempted it had been many years since he had last been hunting and he did not know how his stiff leg would fare. But a drag hunt would not be so bad. He could choose which of the set up obstacles along the trail he would feel able to jump.

"Go on!" Melanie encouraged. You are a fit man and I would feel so much safer with you there. Let's take him to the Blackmoor Estate. If we can get him round there; then he can do anything."

"We'd better get there early then Melanie. You will need to get on this horse at least twenty minutes before anyone else arrives. Let's give him the chance to get used to the environment and see the hounds and other riders as they filter in." Bill knew his boy and wanted Melanie to be safe.

To horse and away. To the heart of the fray!
Fling care to the Devil for the day.
Anonymous

Chapter 3

As night slowly gave way to day the dark scudding clouds took on a pink glow, the tip of a deep red sun creeping up on the far-away horizon. Bill waited tentatively in the yard of the manor holding Running Wind for Melanie as she parked the horsebox. Uncomfortable in his borrowed hacking jacket, Bill was a little nervous. It was still quite dark and very difficult to make out too much detail. "Be careful, Melanie," Bill warned as he gave her a leg up onto the horse, "Remember don't pull on his mouth whatever he does."

Running Wind`s head was high, his ears alert, nostrils flared.

A quieter mid week hunt, thought Melanie *the perfect start for this horse.* As Bill rescued the fat Highland from the lawn before he wrecked it; and stiffly mounted up, Melanie gathered up her reins and hoped she could keep both her wits and her seat on this ride....!

The Lorries started rolling into the yard; black and tweed coated riders unloaded gleaming horses with neat plaited manes and tails.

Bill sat steady on his mount and surveyed the scene. Bertram Highwood the Whipper-in, arrived surrounded by the hounds. Big Blood hounds. Their deep bass voices echoing round the yard. The excited pack seemed unruly but one flick of the whip from Bertram was enough to calm them. Only a couple of wayward youngsters still skipped and barked round him. Sir Dennis Hall rode round the corner on his large, impressive cob. All of 17.1hh the Irish draft cross looked as if it could go through any obstacle it could not jump! Bill had never seen Sir Hall before and it occurred to him that horse and rider were well matched. *He must ride 16 stone at least* thought Bill-as he inwardly smirked!

The huntsman blew his horn gathering the hounds and the Master set off with the rest of the hunt in pursuit. Bill rode alongside Melanie talking to his boy as he went. Fortunately, the Cob Bill was on was an old hand at hunting and dawdled along giving the impression he was only going to run if he really had to. Melanie had her reins loose letting her mount walk easily along breathing deeply to keep herself calm.

They cut out across open country, heading west towards the copse where the dragged trail started. As the field panned out Running Wind, feeling the excitement of the other horses began to prance. Melanie sat deep and still only using movements of her hips to steady him. Suddenly one of the hounds sang out... his snout barely an inch from the ground. The cry taken up by the others- one by one till all fell into full cry. Their deep voices resonating round the valley with age old song. They set off fast, running towards the copse. Blowing his horn hard the Whipper-in rode past Running Wind at a strong canter. Melanie looked sideways at Bill for reassurance just in time to see his "quiet" mount give a huge buck and set off fast after the Whipper-in. Running Wind did a walk to fast canter in one smooth movement, picking up to gallop in two strides as Melanie tried to gather up her long reins. Halfway up the meadow lay a wide open drainage ditch. There was a narrow grassed pathway over it which some of the followers were heading for… but the master and his close members were riding straight at the cavernous ditch. One after another the horses jumped the huge gaping expanse. Bill wanted to lead over the pathway, but his mount had the bit hard in his teeth, making his neck as flexible as a lump of wood!

"We'll have to jump it!" he shouted at Melanie, as Running Wind, the faster horse came level with Bill. Before Melanie could even reply the ditch was before her. Deciding just to trust the horse and his love of jumping she sat quiet and gave him his head. He soared high, clearing the sides easily. Looking back she saw Bill cling to the neck strap and lean forwards as the pony happily leapt over. They then raced on over the rough meadow.

With her heart racing Melanie found that she was actually enjoying the ride more than she had anticipated. She looked down at her horse's neck. Wet foamy sweat darkened his coat and in the cool air she saw steam rising above his neatly plaited mane. *How unbelievably fantastic was this moment in suspended and somehow surreal time!*

The hounds were still baying; in the distance she could just see the Master standing in his stirrups as he cantered along.

They crashed through the woods. The horse's hooves snapping and breaking small branches underfoot. The faster riders had slowed to a trot under the canopy of the trees allowing the tail enders to catch up.

"Whoa, you brute!" Bill admonished his mount as they nearly ran into Running Wind's hind end, who in turn spun round ready to set off again.

"Melanie, where the hell did you get this old cart horse from?"

"Who? Hamish? Oh, just from one of my yard girls! It's her father's old hunting pony. Oh and I don't think he's been out much this last couple of years." she teased!

"Last decade more like," Bill muttered.

Emerging from the woods they saw the hunt spread out in a large field, the front runners already crossing what looked from a distance like a large river.

Melanie slowed as they approached; glad she had been taking Running Wind into the stream near her stables every day this last month in preparation. Confident he would go in she sat quietly and simply asked the horse to cross. When she reached the other side, she turned him to watch how Bill was fairing. Not at all sure of the Highland Bill came at the bank of the river at a fast trot. Hamish looked at first as if he would offer no hesitation, then suddenly he slammed on his brakes... planting both feet. Poor Bill shot out of the saddle upwards and forwards landing back on the horse`s neck which was stretched out over the water. Swallowing her desire to laugh, Melanie watched, fairly sure that the pony would drop his head ducking Bill in. Luckily for Bill, Hamish raised his head pushing his rider upright and stepped backwards away from the river. Somehow Bill managed to scramble back into the saddle just in time as the pony swung round and set off back towards the Manor. Running Wind did not hesitate to re cross the river and follow despite Melanie's attempts to rein him round and re-join the hunt. Mortified she realised that after only 15 minutes going out, they were now on their way home! Optimistically cheered on by a group of spectators standing by their land Rover.

Once he had achieved what he wanted Hamish slowed his pace... not so Running Wind to whom this was just one more race to win.

Oh God thought Melanie, *not only have we abandoned the Hunt, but we are going to arrive across the Manor lawns at a flat out gallop Her heart sank at the embarrassment!*

Unable to slow the horse Melanie could do nothing but sit tight as they swept through the woods once more branches thwacking her face and thudding against her hat. She lay flat on Running Winds neck. He took this as a jockey's signal to go faster and willingly obliged breaking again into a full tilt gallop. Grateful only that they were not galloping past the Master at this speed Melanie heard Bill swearing from somewhere behind.

Running Wind took the on-coming ditch in his stride as if it were not there; he was galloping for sheer joy up the meadow. By this time Bill's mount was blown and had dropped to a trot. Realising his buddy was not with him, Running Wind slowed... turning to look for the pony. The over weight old Highland was walking now his sides heaving, breathing hard from his expansive nostrils. Her mount, Melanie realised, was hardly winded at all and despite being lathered with sweat he seemed fresh enough to start all over again. Rob was right. This was a seriously talented, if somewhat dangerously excitable, horse!

Bill walked so slowly into the yard the next day Melanie had to turn her face away to hide her amusement not wishing to hurt the old man's feelings, *I'll bet you are as stiff as a board and sore* she thought. *Well, at any rate at least you didn't actually fall off. Fair play old friend!*

Cold February mist hung round the stables as Running Wind was quietly loaded into Melanie's trailer. This was to be a very special outing and the preparation for today had been radical to say the least. Although Melanie had rehabilitated many race horses for life outside of racing, she had never even thought of training one or entering a horse for an actual race. However the special character of this horse had led her to try this one race before offering him up for sale. Not only would his price be higher if he did well, but she also had to ensure that his next owner would take Bill as well as the horse.

A few months back when Melanie had described her plan to Bill he had stared at her in disbelief. "We are going to train and enter Running Wind for a point to point and you will ride him?" Bill repeated what she had explained to him slowly so he was sure this was what she wanted. "I groom and look after him, you ride him out on hacks and over your cross country course, nearer the time we take him to a beach once a week to gallop and onto the Wolds once a week. We enter him for a point to point hurdle race over 3 miles 2 furlongs with you as jockey!!"

"Yes –let's face it. We have nothing to lose –if he runs as well as I think he will we will be able to not only name his price but also include you in the package Bill Harding "she added laughing.

"Thank you, milady," Bill joked taking her hand and kissing it.

Holderness was shrouded in grey scudding clouds. It seemed rain was forecast. Secretly Melanie hoped it would rain as Running Wind always seemed to run better when the going was soft. Whilst Bill was leading his boy round the parade ring and Melanie was weighing in Carlie went down to the stands to look at the odds on the on-course betting touts. Standing a little way back from the crowds round the bookie she watched and listened. Betting was in full swing for this open member's race... the Holderness Drag Hound Hunt Cup over 18 fences with 2 wide ditches. The rain had started and was falling steadily. Running Wind had very long odds she saw- 25 to 1. Despite being well known as a runner on the flat, his long absence and reputation as a difficult horse had put off the punters. *Good* she thought! – not one for frequent gambling (but fond of an occasional flutter if she liked the look of a horse,) Carlie put on a giddy bet of £20 to win only, followed by £100 for Melanie and a further £50 for Bill on Running Wind. The plump man in a bearskin hat and thick woolly coat gave her a strange look of surprise mixed with pity, almost as if he did not feel comfortable taking her money....but take it he did!

Under Starter`s orders! Melanie sat quietly on her horse as the starter checked the safety of Running Winds tack. Adrenalin was just beginning to take over from last minute nerves. The horse up on his toes was sweating a little between his hind legs. Bill was happy though, at the behaviour of his boy.

The horses were on their way to the start and Melanie made sure she was tucked in behind the group of other horses. "Well at least there is no gate this time." Bill had said when they were in the planning stages. Indeed Melanie thought this whole set up of running over fences for a long distance suited her horse very well.

Melanie had some work to do to keep her mount calm before the start, as the field were milling around. The signal was given to prepare, as the horses rounded the barrier and then suddenly they were off. Thirteen horses pounding down that hallowed grass towards the first fence. Carlie was clutching so hard to her tote tickets she knew that this was it.... The big test if Running Wind could jump as well in the race as he always did at home she thought his chances of winning were very good .*Go on Mel!*

Running Wind was second from last as they approached the first obstacle, the birch fence of 4 foot 6 inches high gently sloping away from the on-coming horses. Melanie steadied her mount several strides out and then decided to let the horse see his own stride. Watching the front horse's jump Melanie was again aware of how important it was that the horse took off well, cleared the jump and landed easily, thus attaining a few strides on any clumsy horse that jumped badly or struck the jump. His ears pricked Running Wind soared over the jump and much to Melanie's amusement was squealing as he ran on. They had gained three places already with this first jump so she gently asked for a little more. Over the next 4 fences they gained another 5 places. The five horses ahead were quite closely bunched up.... *Perfect!* Melanie thought... *to keep this strong horse in check for her!* As Bill had told her countless times never to pull hard on his mouth. "That's how Rob won so many races on the boy -- never pulling." So Melanie decided to keep to the outside and avoid the rails. Luckily, they were not too close to the front runners as the favourite fell at the next fence nearly unseating the jockey on the second placed horse. Running Wind ignored the fallen jockey and the horse struggling, unhurt, to his feet. However this left an open gap as he took the next hurdle with similar easy grace. Running Wind landed very well and what happened next was really quite simple. The horse took the bit raised his head and was off! *Oh God* thought Melanie, *here we go again*. Just as he had done on their first hunt outing Running Wind was indeed just simply running. *A passenger...that's all I am! Well at least we are still going fast in the right direction and can this horse jump!* At the next fence they approached level with the chestnut Fire Island who took the jump lurching to the side. Running Wind`s perfect style jumped him into second place and Melanie was vaguely aware of the cheering of the crowd, still sure that Murky Waters would win. They were level running when jumping the second from last which just left the final run down the long straight to the final fence. Running Wind landed brilliantly so well in fact that he was suddenly half a length ahead. He so easily followed up his advantage; Melanie had absolutely no hold what so ever on this horse. He was simply flying towards the post. Switching allegiance the crowds were now cheering the slight woman on the bay horse as he ate up the ground, in huge easy strides. Several yards before the post Melanie had already raised her arm.

Carlie had the dignity to look beyond the bookie as he dealt out her winnings, *A few glasses of champagne tonight,* she thought. *FANTASTIC!*

"No!" Melanie was determined. "I will not sell him without a written understanding that Bill goes with him as his groom. If you cannot understand how important this is you will never win any races with this horse."

"You are a very persuasive young lady!" Peter Lake sighed, not used to having a woman telling him what to do. "Is this groom, this Bill... really so important?"
"Yes, I can tell you Running Winds whole life history if you want and you will understand." Melanie was adamant "In fact I think you should call Desmond Wilks before you even consider taking this horse."

Peter was reflective. His habit of always video recording any races he attended had, for some reason, also applied to this small time Point to Point his friend Colin James had persuaded him to come to. He had replayed and watched Running Wind's spectacular win so many times and each time he had been impressed at the horses jumping ability and commitment to the race. Whatever happened around him he kept his focus and concentrated on his job! Peter did not miss that the jockey, Melanie Watson, had simply been a passenger and that the horse had won the race on his own. If the price of acquiring this promising horse was an additional somewhat aged lad then so be it. He desperately needed a good winning horse. His stables were not what they used to be as several owners had moved on to the bigger yards. Because Melanie was so insistent that the only way she would sell was if Bill went too, the price of this horse was within Peter's budget. Selling off the home farm attached to his property was, he knew, not a good thing for the yard, but it would allow him not only to buy Running Wind, but also settle his debt with Joe Brookes, the bookmakers.

At 58 he knew he was nearing the end of his training career and that big win had always evaded him. He closed his eyes and saw again his lifetime dream of picking up the Gold Cup.

Unimpressed with the small damp apartment above the stables which had been allocated to him, Bill was none the less pleased with the yard. The stables were clean and spacious and the paddocks were well fenced. He had heard rumours that Peter Lake was in financial difficulties caused by his gambling, but there was no sign of that so far as Bill could see. Although Running Wind had not sold for top price, he had still not come cheap. Could this be it? Bill knew already that Peter intended to bring the horse on slowly through several races this year and next year. His ambition was Cheltenham. Well, nothing would please Bill more than seeing his boy win the Gold Cup.

Ballet technique is arbitrary and very diffi-
cult- it never becomes easy it becomes
possible.
Agnes de Lille

Chapter 4 (thirteen years earlier)

"Papa Papa PAPA"! --- Natalie called.

Shuffling in his slippers, like an old man, he came from the kitchen.

She held out the letter to her father which he took in his shaking hands.

Even after 20 years in England the written word was still sometimes difficult for him. Slowly he deciphered the words.

It was hard to believe. They were offering Natalie a place at the Barbican Ballet School in London, an aided place. If he could find £267 per year she could have nearly thirty thousand pounds worth of schooling boarding and medical cover per year.

"I've done it papa!! They want me--- my dream- come true!" Natalie cried as she danced round her Father--- then as if thinking of something, she stopped.

"Oh but papa---- you will be all alone." she looked up at him with her large Hazel eyes.

"Ah no Natalie. No, your mother would have been so proud of you; her greatest desire was that you should dance-- it was her life."

As Natalie skipped off happily with her letter Johan Diaz reflected on all of this. Although he was nearly 60 Natalie was only 11, he had done just about as much as he could for his kind, gentle and talented daughter. Long hours in his woodwork shop had weakened his lungs and on his last visit the doctor had told him he did not have much time left. Harsh wracking cough's left him weak in the morning and it was proving increasingly difficult to hide his state of health from his daughter. She would be well looked after, educated and, most importantly schooled in ballet –if he was going to be lonely and miss her terribly, it was small price to pay for this miraculous gift. She would have a family of sorts to care for her when he was gone –he only hoped he could see her really perform just one time. With great sadness he remembered his wife's last words "I will never see it Johan, but if she wishes it, please let her dance." Despite all his misgivings about this demanding profession he had promised his dying wife to do everything in his power to help Natalie. It had been only by chance one of his clients had mentioned that a friends daughter had won a scholarship to a ballet school, setting Johan writing letters to every top ballet establishment. This offer of a place at one of the best was the reward for all his efforts taking Natalie to audition.

Natalie at 11 could not have begun to understand how much money £ 267 was to her father.

Johan was still reflecting upon exactly how he could find such a sum when the phone rang – Mr Briggs his most demanding client asking for more done yesterday as usual.

"The chairs are fine Mr Diaz, but I need six more by Tuesday." He rasped into the phone. At 7.00 pm on a Friday night, this would mean Johan working all weekend –always in need of money he would normally agree without conditions. This time though something seemed to shift inside him and as if from a distance he heard himself saying –"Ah I have a prior order this weekend Mr Briggs." He could almost feel the surprised frustration down the line as the bullying Briggs realised that Johan had some spunk after all. "Well I am prepared to pay a little extra –I need to have them." Briggs sounded exasperated. This was the first time the weedy little woodworker had proposed such a thing. Johan decided to go for broke –"I will have to have £250 extra to cover the payment I will lose" he replied. Briggs did not miss a beat –"OK but I will pick them up Monday morning." – Johan knew he had a long hard weekend ahead –but he had done it; he could afford Natalie's course fees now.

Through out the long journey South by train Natalie had chatted animatedly with her father about what the school would be like lessons, friends, learning new ballet steps, performing maybe for the school, but now in the taxi from the station she fell silent as if the full realisation of what she was doing had hit her. Soon –too soon- her father would leave her in a strange place, full of strange people. Her mood affected her father and he too fell silent gazing out of the windows at London. The black cab swept up a long tree lined drive and Natalie saw the magnificent Colonial building for the first time, opposite the lovely Hyde Park, the elegant former Mansion belonging to a Raj of the British Empire was impressive. Abundant yellow lilies and aromatic herb bushes decorated the grounds softening the lines of a building which could easily have been oppressive and a graceful fountain played charmingly just in front of the stone steps leading to the door. A slim woman dressed elegantly in black and white, her hair in a neat chignon stood at the bottom of the flight of steps.

Natalie would have remained at the door long after her father's taxi had disappeared, but Isobel Courtin knew that the best cure for the normal distress and homesickness which hit the new young students was bustling activity in these strange surroundings.

"Come now. We will take a tour around and get you settled in," she soothed passing Natalie a fragrant handkerchief. "Then you can meet the others. "

Although she had seen a couple of photos of the school in the brochure, Natalie had not expected the grandeur of this lovely building with arched high windows which gave plenty of light. They looked into studios and watched some of the students; boys in blue tight jump suits and the girls in pink leotards and grey tights at their lessons. Climbing a staircase with fabulous wrought iron railings they were passed by a group of chattering girls about Natalie's age wearing black track suits. As they passed a lovely painting of an elegant and beautiful ballerina each performed an elegant curtsey. Fascinated Natalie looked up at Mme Courtin who smiled down –"It is believed to give good luck to curtsey before the image of `Darcy Bustle'."she explained – "go on you too," she encouraged, laughing as Natalie went back down the stairs and nervously performed her own, very graceful, homage to the heroine.

The level of noise that assailed Natalie's ears as they entered the refractory was decibels above anything she had ever encountered before with so many children aged from 11 to 16 all seeming to speak at once, Natalie winced not only from the sounds but also the smells of this huge room which were completely alien and alarming to her. The primary school Natalie had attended had been only a 10 minute walk from her home, Johan would quit his workshop which was their garage attached to the house and walk to the school to fetch her for a lunch at home. Never in her life had she been inside a canteen like this.

Natalie felt her shoulder being pushed from behind as Isobel Courtin herded her towards the queue lining up trays in hand, with a plastic screen to their side behind which three matronly looking women were serving what looked to Natalie to be huge helpings of unidentifiable food. Her look of incredulity was taken by her Tutor as pleased surprise, and Isobel forced her to the end of the queue putting a tray containing a glass and a knife and fork into her hands.

"You can eat what you wish my dear, so ask for anything which takes your fancy" Turning round to survey the room – she motioned to one of the tables "Brenda Williams come over here and help our new recruit settle in."

A sulky faced girl stood up and started walking over.

"Right I will see you in an hour's time Natalie and we will meet your House mistress." With that she turned on her heels and walked away.

"Old Cottage Drape taking you round herself is she –oh we must be a promising little miss." Brenda gave Natalie a thump on her back which could have been intended to be chummy, but for the sheer force behind it.

Overwhelmed Natalie was close to tears. A quiet soft voice asked her

"Your turn my dear what will it be? " Joan Simpson had a daughter of about Natalie's age at home who was shy – so she felt sympathy for the girl.

Bewildered by the array of steaming containers, she turned her eyes to the kind face above her; close to panic she was speechless.

Sensing her dismay Joan coaxed "How about a little of the quiche with a baked potato and salad." Quickly she piled a plate with a tasty looking quiche. Carefully she selected a small potato, seeing Natalie's size and apprehension and a little side salad and poured water into her glass, eager to push Natalie on as a crowd of hungry youngsters having bolted their first course, were looking greedily at the puddings.

All the girls at the table looked up to watch Natalie as she sat down. Brenda slumped into the seat next to her.

"Term started a week ago. Where you have been" asked another girl, pretty, her silky blonde hair tied back in by a rose pink ribbon.

"My father was ill and could not bring me until now. "

Seeing Natalie's look of distress the girl reassured her – "My name is Amanda and I only started today – we were away in Kuala Lumpur with daddy's work and just flew back." Amanda chatted on amicably about life in Malaysia.

Having eaten about half the food on her plate and then pushed it away, Natalie realised she was being watched –Brenda had a coveting look on her face.

"Are you going to eat the rest or just look at it? "

"Why? Would you like to eat the rest? "Natalie watched horrified as Brenda dragged her plate over and with gobbling motions speedily emptied the plate. "Right, let's get dessert now!" Brenda stated, rising as she spoke and hurrying back over.

"Not for me," Natalie replied.

Brenda turned round and spat back at Natalie, "We are only allowed one each; I will eat yours- go and get one. Make sure it has chocolate on it."

As she walked round with Mme Courtin later Natalie felt nauseous and more than once thought she would actually be sick. Although the food had been tasty, the smells in the canteen and the sight of Brenda shovelling in mouthful after mouthful of the two puddings had been to her, disgusting. Realisation struck her that she was not going to enjoy everything about her new life. Food had never been important in her life and she was not looking forward to eating three times a day in such circumstances. Another aspect was Brenda's bullying ways –Natalie decided to avoid her as much as possible, amazed that such a greedy girl should be here at all. Natalie did not know it, but Brenda was unlikely to survive the first assessment which would ensure that only the really good talented girls went through to the next year.

Loneliness gave way to exhaustion and exhilaration as Natalie began her journey to become the prima ballerina she aspired to be. Isobel Courtin saw she had a supremely talented young girl in Natalie and worked her accordingly. The fact that Natalie's father was unable to visit regularly as most parents did meant that Natalie relied even more on her tutor than most of the pupils. Accustomed to hard work Natalie pleased her new family more than she ever really knew.

A few weeks after Natalie had joined the school an event occurred that was eagerly awaited by the girls, something they had each been dreaming about for years, the arrival of their first point shoes. Although the girls were not supposed to get up on their points until their bones were strong enough; the wrappings were quickly torn off the delicate pink shoes and the girls all tried standing on them for the first time.

Natalie felt as if she was floating when she rose up, delicate as a blade of grass. She had a lovely feeling inside of being at peace and able to express herself at last. A loud thump heralded the first casualty as Brenda came down heavily and stumbled over. One by one the girls had to descend and admit defeat. Long after all the rest had succumbed Natalie stood on seeming to be in a trance, oblivious to any pain.

When Isobel overheard some of the girls discussing the day the shoes came and how Natalie had stood on alone and did not seem to be feeling the same pain and imbalance that they were, she smiled to herself. Not for the first time her instinct, felt when she watched Natalie's audition, was a good one. This was to be a girl to watch.

Choosing which of the young new ballerinas were to feature in the productions which the ballet school gave every year , was always difficult and places were much coveted by the young "stars ". The choice of Natalie for Giselle was not popular among the pupils – new, shy, and not at all one of the groups, Natalie was subsequently ostracized by her peers. For most normal young girls this would have been distressing, but Natalie's life had been far from normal and, although you could not say she was completely unaware of the situation, it did not cause her undue grief. She was to throw herself into the training with relish. It seemed to Isobel that the more work she gave the girl, the better she enjoyed it. Young Natalie was so very slim and willowy bending like an elegant tree in the wind. Her pure grace and natural talent, which had led to her selection, pleased the often taciturn Mme Courtin.

Only Amanda had the generosity of heart to be genuinely pleased for Natalie, but then Amanda had also been picked to perform and the two girls spent a lot of time at the rehearsals together matched well not only in age but also size and proportions.

Natalie was alone, standing again up on her points. She had been practising nearly every day recently and could manage to remain still and upright for longer and longer stretches. Holding her breath she was counting the seconds. Brenda looked in and seeing Natalie upright by the door swung her weight onto the handle and pushed –the door crashed into Natalie knocking her over, Brenda then put her weight behind the door and pushed again. Natalie cried out in pain.

"Oh – sorry Natalie," Brenda said "I had no idea you were behind the door – "Are you OK? "

Holding her ankle Natalie looked up at the triumphant Brenda, but said nothing. The final dress rehearsal for Giselle was in two days time. Natalie in tune with her body knew that her leg was badly damaged and she was afraid she would not be able to dance.

"I'm sorry Natalie but we simply cannot permit you to dance at all not even in the chorus "Mme Courtin looked sternly at her young protégé. "Really, how you could have been standing up on your points at all- never mind just before a show. You must learn some decorum." Squashed Natalie realised that Brenda had succeeded.

Her part as Giselle would be taken by Amanda.

The friendship between Natalie and Amanda survived Natalie's removal from the show. Sometimes the girls were allowed some free time in the early summer evenings. Amanda drew Natalie aside –"well have you brought some food?"

"Yes-but why?"

"We are going for a picnic in Hyde Park this evening, –its ok I asked Mme Courtin for permission" she added seeing Natalie's reserve.

With shining eyes the two set towards the arched gate which gave onto the romantic park. Settled under a tree they had a marvellous view of everyone who passed by.

"We could be really in the countryside –not in the middle of London" Amanda remarked.

Natalie agreed with her companion almost overwhelmed by the sight of the beautiful lush park. Originally a private hunting

Estate for Henry VIII the Park had been opened to the public in 1637.

They sat on the grass and ate. Amanda had brought some fruit cake her mother had sent, "Cooks speciality. Try some."

Natalie lost as to what to bring had approached Joan Simpson who had made some tiny, but fresh and delicious sandwiches. They had fresh orange juice to drink and apples in their basket.

Suddenly Amanda nudged Natalie.

"Look! Horses aren't they beautiful?"

The pair had unintentionally sat down on Rotton Row once used as a Royal approach where people still ride their horses.

Natalie turned to see, four huge animals were approaching walking fast, their hooves clopping on the path. The front horse was a fiery reddish colour, the riders looking past the girls seated on the ground with haughty distain.

"The grey is an Arab" Amanda informed Natalie, I had lessons for four years- my favourite was a grey like her. Natalie stood up to see better; she was entranced watching the horses.

As the women riding increased their pace to a trot, she saw the horse Amanda had called an Arab start to float; it's legs rising in high elegant movements, tossing it's head and arching its neck -with its dapple grey body, pure white flashing tail and dark mane and legs it was a stunning beast, Natalie fell in love at first sight.

"Oh, watch the chestnut how he extends his legs!" Amanda enthused. Natalie was lost to the grey, however, and the sight of these magnificent animals as they passed not even paying attention to the girls was to live with Natalie for years.

Inevitably, Brenda failed to make the required grade at the end of the first year. On hearing this news Natalie had a rush of only one emotion, relief. Freed from her overpowering bully Natalie truly loved the next five years of her training.

"Now, girls, we reach a milestone in your dance schooling" Isobel Courtin addressed the 20 girls of 16 who had survived the yearly assessments. "Today you will be appointed a boy partner." Natalie was filled with anguish and anticipation...all young trainee girls knew that their eventual destination was to dance with a male partner but until they mastered their own balance and control adding the difficult dimension of another body and its balance waited. The moment had however, arrived, and Natalie was both eager and apprehensive. Reading from a list Isobel looked up in Natalie's direction "Natalie Diaz and Shaun Falcon, Amanda Brotherly and Gavin Paterson."
Her tutor read on but Natalie stood entranced, Shaun was widely acknowledged by the pupils as the most talented boy in the school – to be partnered with Shaun she knew was an accolade in itself. Her stomach churning with nerves Natalie came forward and took Shaun's out stretched hand.

Finding balance by yourself is one thing. As a pair everything changes completely. Natalie found that if Shaun was even slightly out of tune with her while she was on her points –not holding her quite square, it could cause her pain and strain. Nervous of complaining or seeming weak at first Natalie said nothing. Shaun was not the best student without merit; he sensed Natalie's discomfort and distress.

Suddenly he put his partner down and pushed her away from him.

"OK Natalie what's wrong- and before you say nothing I know something is so pipe up."

Unable to dissemble Natalie confessed how any slight unbalance or unevenness between them could cause her aches and discomfort. Almost immediately Shaun's eyes brightened as soon as he knew what was wrong he could correct it.

"Beginning now we will do all exercises together, bending, stretching, bars. We will learn to become as one."

After a month Natalie knew she was the luckiest girl in the school. Not only was Shaun the most talented dancer but his wonderful idea about them joining as two halves of a whole was an overwhelming success. When the music started the two young bodies responded in total unison.

Watching one day Isobel realised she had never in her life seen a pairing which worked so well.

The School had decided to put on *Romeo and Juliet* this year as their main event. Of course the choice of the lead roles was Isobel's but no one could have chosen other than Natalie and Shaun.

"All right, everyone that's enough for today." Isobel's announcement was greeted by a sigh of relief as the exhausted young students started to go through their after work stretches.

Shaun looked down at Natalie. Although he was not tall Natalie was so petit he seemed to tower above her. "Are you ok Nat?" Concern showed in his eyes he saw how very pale and tired she was. Beads of sweat stood out on Natalie's forehead and there were dark rings under her eyes. "No I'm fine Shaun don't fuss." Taking her by the arm he headed for the door " Hey come and eat then, I'm starving they have put on an extra spread for us, to give us strength for tomorrows show-l bet" he laughed. Nearly too weak to answer, Natalie shook her head – "I'll catch a sandwich later."

"Come on Nat – you have to eat I've been with you all day. You've eaten nothing but an apple and an orange."
Beginning to get angry now, Natalie raised her voice. "Didn't you hear me I'm not hungry."

"Hah suit yourself." Wounded Shaun strode off leaving Natalie alone in the room. Now she had hurt Shaun's feelings, she felt so bereft already missing his company. Often during the night she would fantasise about being kissed by Shaun, held tenderly in his strong arms. When she conjured up these images her pulse started to race and her face felt hot as the imagined kiss went on; she arched her light young body under the bed clothes yearning for an unknown and still unimagined pleasure.

Shaun had not hesitated to pay more attention to Natalie after this and with his gentle encouragement and help from Isobel Courtin. Natalie was guided away from a possible dangerous indifference to food.

Her love for her studies and also Shaun helped her settle and turn away from neglecting her body's needs. Dancing gave her a supreme level of personal concentration but, she was not aware, it also enslaved her. Isobel strove to keep her talent and hard work from becoming an obsession.

Excitement was rising in Natalie. The intoxicating aromas of stage make up, powder and even sweat making her flare her nostrils. This was it-- her first real performance.

Amanda peeped into Natalie's dressing room her eyes shining bright she held out her hand to Natalie. Two small green pills lay there. Shaking her head Natalie shuddered looking at them." No, Amanda, I don't want to take them!"

"Go on, Natalie, you look tired they will help you get through," Amanda encouraged. A recent conversation with Shaun had touched on the subject of drugs and his horror of them." I am going to eat some fruit and yoghurt instead."

Amanda's look of scorn and scepticism, as she left to dress, was not lost on Natalie. Nothing was going to spoil this precious moment. How wonderful to play Juliet to Shaun's Romeo- in the annual school matinee.

Nothing in Natalie's life and schooling had truly prepared her for the feelings she had waiting to go on stage. Her heart felt as if it was skipping every second beat and she had swallows not butterflies in her stomach. She knew the auditorium was full;

this was the most important moment of her career the position of chorus dancer at the prestigious Barbican Ballet Co would be filled today. Natalie was expected to get this post but the experts had to be convinced. Everyone who was anyone in the ballet world would be there watching her. The music picked up the tempo and she heard her cue –a surge of adrenalin propelled her onto the stage high on her points as she twirled towards Shaun –he swept her elegantly up wards over his head. She felt as if she was floating on air; muscle to muscle, skin to skin the pair looked indeed like two halves of a whole. Natalie felt as if their breaths were one breath, their hearts beating in total harmony. Silence had fallen over the audience watching them dance, then a collective gasp. This thing, this being which they knew was two young dancers was spell binding, amazing! Startling images of the pair so matched as they rose and fell, joined and parted like wild horses in a herd as they moved in unison would remain in the minds of the spectators forever.

Isobel was waiting for Natalie in the wings, watching as she picked up the flowers strewn across the stage, full of emotion and fierce pride.

Still carried high on adrenalin Natalie ran off the stage into Isobel's arms "My dear you have surpassed even my highest hopes. That was one of the most wonderful performances I have ever seen. Congratulations on two counts I can confirm your place at the Barbican Ballet Co."

Stunned with tears glinting in her eyes Natalie hugged her protector and advisor for the last 6 years unable to utter more than a choked thank you.

"I will introduce you to the Principal at the party. Now go and have a bath and get changed."

Sitting on the edge of the bath Amanda looked lovely if somewhat thin, her long blonde hair swept up on her head, held there with a golden clasp. *Real gold* Natalie thought. Amanda's father she realised was seriously rich. With no rich father to buy her a dress Natalie had not been looking forward to the ball, until this morning when a long slim box had arrived. Inside she had found the most beautiful deep green silk dress, a pair of elegant heeled shoes in the same emerald colour and a cortege of yellow and white flowers. The simple white card said only, "With my love, Shaun."

No wonder they had danced so well together. Natalie was on cloud nine *"my love"* Shaun had actually written of his love for her.

"Two tendrils of hair one each side casually falling, there-very sensual!" Amanda said teasing her friend as she put the finishing touches to her coiffure.

For the second time in one evening Natalie felt as if she was floating. She glided down the stairs and it seemed as if the whole college was waiting at the bottom for her. Shaun was standing at the foot of the stairs at his side Claude Grant; stunningly handsome with deep blue eyes, his soft fair hair was longer than Amanda's. Claude whistled as Natalie shyly thanked Shaun for his generous and thoughtful present." I told you it would go with her eyes" Claude squeezed Shaun's arm "Exactly the same shade as the green in the middle, darling "He pouted liked a girl "Couldn't even remember what colour of eyes you have- dippy boy." Claude looked adoringly at Shaun. Startled Natalie asked "You were there when he bought it? "

"There darling! – It was my idea-- to thank you for lifting his star – now we will both go to Covent Garden together." As he spoke he curled his arm round Shaun and led him off "Come on gorgeous let's charge your energy for tonight."

Amanda took Natalie's arm and held her up --she looked about to collapse.

Panicked that Natalie was about to bolt –Amanda steered her quickly past Isobel who raised her eyes in question. She was standing next to the Principal of the Barbican ballet Co who was keen to meet the stars. "Just freshening up" said Amanda lightly.

In the toilets she turned to face her friend, Natalie was ashen and trembling.

"Oh God I am so stupid –did you know Amanda?" White-faced Natalie whispered to her friend.

"Well I knew about Claude. Every girl in the school wants him and he's not interested. I had my suspicions about Shaun, but he did seem keen on you."

Adrian Ravenscroft lifted the two drinks he had just bought at the bar high above the crowd in the pub and made his way to the elegant figure waiting at a table.

"So Isobel you want to know how our little star is doing" as he spoke he laid the two glasses of gin and tonic on the table."Well, her dancing is superb. I cannot fault it and she certainly draws the crowds they love her, but her health seems very delicate, I had the impression she was very distressed about something at first." He paused and took a sip from his drink, "It took her a good six months to seem truly relaxed and happy."

Isobel left her own drink untouched as if it was incidental to the meeting "How does she seem now 18 months on?"

"Thankfully she seems to have settled down and is much happier, "Adrian replied. "I can't say I am impressed by her recent choice of boyfriend though."

Isobel leant forward "What do you mean?" For the first time in her career she had allowed herself to become emotionally involved with a pupil. Childless she had really taken to the lonely Natalie even after all this time she still worried about her best ever protégé.

"Well that young man she has been seeing – he was thrown out of Choreography school and seems to be a drop out in every way. "

For a very long time Natalie stared at the card in her hand. It was from the electricity board. They had cut off the supply to the flat. Natalie knew she had given Stefan the money for these bills – she saw the last two had not been paid at all and there was a final demand for the rent –this she had also given to Stefan to pay. Natalie was in a reflective mood. In the last two years since she had been with Stefan she knew she had been giving him more and more money – he claimed the bills were increasing and that he earned next to nothing as a choreographic student. The reality Natalie now saw was that other members of the company, even those much more junior than she, lived well and many had mortgages on properties of their own. Starkly aware that in her dependant naivety since her father's death; she had just left all the finances to Stefan. Natalie realised that despite her earning a very good wage as principle ballerina for the company, she still lived in the same dingy flat with no views and shabby furniture. At 22 she knew she was young to be so senior in the company, but her fathers death nearly two years ago had been the supreme catalyst for her career. She remembered his one visit south to see her dance; her visits home in the last years had been few and it had been 18 months since she had last made the trip. Shocked she saw an old and very thin man –the ghostly relic of her father as she remembered him, wracked by a harsh rattling cough he seemed weak; too frail to remain standing for long.

Natalie would never know how much effort it cost Johan to undertake the trip, but he just had to see her dance once more before he died. Natalie's best memory was seeing him afterwards his eyes tearful, but full of poignant tender pride.

The door slammed! Natalie heard the fridge door open then close; when she entered the kitchen Stefan was leaning on the fridge with a bottle of beer in his hand. His hair fell forward over his forehead. He was handsome with a finely carved face, and an elegant slim form, but his tallow skin and a tendency to frown kept him from being classically good looking.

"What happened to the lights?" he said in the dusky gloom.

"The power has been cut off! Stefan....they say we have not paid the last two bills and the rent is way over due – I gave you the money for these bills. Where has it gone Stefan? What is happening?" Natalie's voice was querulous.

Stefan flung himself round to fully face her - fury flashing in his eyes-"What do you mean? I buy the food, don't I?"

"No, Stefan- I have been doing the shopping with the small amount of money I do not give you –Why have the bills not been paid and how many other bills do we owe?" Her increasing anger was resonant in her words.

"Oh listen to Miss Prim – why don't you ask for a rise? We need more money." Stefan replied petulantly.

"Stefan... I was given a rise only 5 months ago! We should have more than enough with your wages on top, to live well."

"That's right. Blame me for it all. Just because I do not earn as much as you." Stefan's voice was childish and resentful.

"But where has the money gone Stefan? We hardly ever eat out and I always pay when we do. I buy very little for myself." Natalie replied her voice choked, she was close to tears.

"Oh poor little girl! Well this poor man needs a drink. I am going out!" Stefan spat the last words in her direction.

As she heard the door slam for the second time Natalie realised that not only was Stefan not being honest with her but that there were probably many more debts she did not yet know about. For the first time she was really grateful to Jeremy Castle for his advice. When her father died Jeremy, her father's friend and their family lawyer had suggested that Natalie put the proceeds from the sale of his house (Natalie's family home) into a high interest account for two years. With the money tied up so she could not touch it. The 24 months were nearly up and Natalie had planned to give Stefan a surprise by telling him of this investment – something had always kept her from telling him before and he knew nothing about it. Nor shall he she resolved. This was her parents hard earned money --her money and not to be squandered. She was sure her father would have wanted her to use the money to make her life better. Fortunately, Natalie had no records of this money at home: Jeremy had suggested that it was easier if it was all kept in the Firms safe and she could access it at any time through Marjorie Evans, the Firm secretary who had also known Natalie for many years, and they sometimes met for a coffee and chat. Natalie now wondered if they had not actually suggested this to protect her from Stefan – he had not been popular with many of her friends and most had drifted away.

"Concentration, Natalie!" – Ivan Shingler called—"What is it with you today? I have never known you so distracted. The first night is in two weeks."

Natalie felt weak. She had not eaten properly for some weeks since she discovered about Stefan and the bills. She had found out bit by bit that they were quite heavily in debt and she was unsure as to what to do.

Stefan's behaviour was erratic, aggressive and bullying. Yesterday she had found a small packet containing white powder in the pocket of a pair of Stefan's jeans she was about to wash. Unsure what to do about it and afraid to confront him she simply put the packet back and stuffed the jeans deep into the dirty washing bin. Later she had heard Stefan frantically sorting through the bin and finally up ending it. He left with a loud crash of the door leaving the laundry spread all over the kitchen floor.

The ballet her company were preparing to do was Swan Lake, a very demanding one and her part was not easy to perform. Her worries about the lies and threats from Stefan and their finances was not helping, she passed many hours of the day worrying, a new and domineering emotion.

As soon as she realised what was happening Natalie ceased giving Stefan her money. He was incensed, furious and increasingly aggressive, Natalie felt almost afraid of him as he became more and more threatening.

"I have to have money now, Natalie" he pleaded.

"What for Stefan? I am paying the bills now with the little money I have we are so behind, where did all this money go? – What did you spend it on?"

His curt reply to this was unusual as Stefan had become morose and often did not speak to Natalie for days.

"Shut up you stupid bitch! You know nothing!" As usual he banged out of the flat. Natalie knew she would not see him until the next day at the earliest.

Sometimes Natalie was physically sick, not only at the thought of Stefan's behaviour, but also because she was now taking several pills every day to help her through, including thyroid tablets.

Natalie had lost over 1 stone in weight in the last 8 months. Never tending to putting on weight she was truly underweight and struggling with the energy and strength needed for her role. In fact she often had to lie down in the changing room between performances. In all her life Natalie hadn't given in, following the example and desires of her hardworking parents. She willingly pushed herself beyond her limits and she was determined to dance well on stage with this performance.

Although some of the other dancers on the cast were aware that Natalie was not her usual self – because of her natural reticence they were all truly unaware of her true problems and state of health. Make up covered the worst of her illness. Always pretty her face was now a bit too thin and angular. But ballet dancers are usually thin and her fellow cast members did not look too closely at someone who had never really been one of the gang.

The worries about finances and debts and Stefan's betrayal and behaviour had eaten into Natalie's defences and composure. She was seriously under weight and becoming anorexic. Ballerinas are by nature slim and supple and fit but Natalie's fat ratio was way too low and she was in danger as she asked her body for more and more in this demanding role.

Natalie was however truly unaware of how much strain she was putting daily on her body, the smaller signs such as her hair thinning and her periods stopping were obvious to her, but she was totally unaware of the problems she was creating for her heart and cardiac system. The matinee seemed to have exhausted her more than usual and Natalie went into her dressing room and sank onto the chaise-longue which had been placed there. She knew she should eat something and a range of sandwiches and a bowl of fruit were on her dressing table. The only thing Natalie picked up was the bottle of spring water – she drained the contents and sank back dozing. Startled Natalie realised that the stage hand was calling and the evening performance would start soon. She had slept for two hours, but she did feel better. Swan Lake had always been the one ballet she really wanted to perform the lead in – her mother had always spoken of this particular ballet with great affection and regret as she had never played the lead role.

Natalie looked at her diary, *week 17* she sighed to herself *only 9 weeks left then maybe I can have a rest*. From inside her diary she took a very old black and white photo. Although the print was creased and a little faded, the lines of the elegant but petit ballerina with such poise and strength were clear enough, showing her mother up on her points with her arms arched above her head. A lone tear dropped onto the photo as Natalie reflected that Stella Diaz had not lived to see her daughter dance. *I am doing it for you*, she whispered to the image.

When the curtain rose, however, a wave of tiredness and nausea washed over Natalie gritting her teeth she went out on stage and for the first act put in a fair performance. Act 2 was the most demanding where Odette made her spectacular entrance. Natalie could feel the sweat running between her shoulder blades and on her forehead as she danced onto the stage; every muscle in her body was taut as she glided across the wooden floor, bending and spiralling up on her points. Odette swayed towards and away from Siegfried. As he held her to him for the third time Ryan Salter heard her gasp. "I can't –oh god, Ryan hold me." Natalie could feel her heart beating so fast and hard as if it would burst. There was terrible pain in her chest. Ryan held her for longer than normal then gently set her on her feet – instead of spiralling away on her points however, Natalie collapsed onto the floor like a deflating balloon. Ryan rushed back to her, as the stage manager signalled the dropping of the curtain. A few of the audience thought this was part of the ballet, but most knew Swan Lake well and were aware that this was unusual. With a soft swish the curtain descended blocking the scene from the audience. Backstage all was chaos. An ambulance was called and the theatre doctor ran to the stage, quickly realising that Natalie had had a cardiac arrest. He started to push rhythmically on her chest to keep the oxygenated blood pumping round the vital organs and, most importantly, her brain.

Rushed to St John's Hospital Natalie's condition was serious and she was in intensive care for 3 days. Finally past the crisis she was in a private ward although she herself was unaware that she was receiving special treatment as she had only been in a hospital once before when summoned to her fathers death bed.

Outside her room two Doctors were in serious discussions about Natalie, Dr Noble handed Dr Jennifer Swann the case notes " I agree with you Jennifer. It looks like she has Anorexia Nervosa. We need to try to find out the root cause and give her the support she needs, but she is so reluctant to really speak with anyone."

"That said- the risks are real – her heart going into cardiac arrest again or internal organ failure, "Dr Swann continued.

"Our job is to try to help her to find a permanent solution to her problem which is causing this mental scarring and self abuse" replied Dr Noble. "First we have to get her to want to eat. She is refusing all food."

"We really do need to get her to talk to someone" Jennifer sighed. "Has she no family or friends? No one seems to visit her."

He just sets off towards the fences and invites you to throw your spirit with him.
Bourgh Scott

Chapter 5

Natalie was aware that someone was in the room with her –
"Stefan," she whispered.

"No, Natalie it's me Jeremy."

Slowly through a fuzzy haze Natalie became aware that it was indeed Jeremy sitting beside her. He was gently holding her hand. His clear blue eyes looking anxiously into hers. Wearing as he always did a tweed suit and a bow tie, he looked much older than his age which she knew was 36. A full head of foppish blonde hair softened what might have been an intimidating appearance. Awkwardly he handed her a beautiful bouquet of flowers. The coloured blooms seemed huge in her tiny bony hand. Jeremy searched the bathroom and reappeared with a plastic jug full of water in which he carefully arranged the flowers, giving Natalie time to adjust to his arrival.

"Oh Jeremy... how good of you to come and see me." She sounded groggy. The medical staff had warned him she was sedated.

As if to avoid any awkward questions Jeremy started talking about the weather and whether it would hold for the next week.

Thrown by this dissembling Natalie was drawn into conversation.

"Why what happens next week?"

"My horse Duplex runs in the Cheltenham Gold Cup for the first time."

"You have a horse?" Natalie was amazed.

"Yes a race horse and she has quite good odds for the Gold Cup. She runs on Friday, at Cheltenham and, I would like you to come with me to watch her run, if you are well enough" – Jeremy had already spoken with the doctors about this idea and they confirmed that Natalie's problem was mostly her worries and that well looked after by Jeremy there was no reason she could not go. Even better maybe Jeremy could find out what was really troubling her.

Without thinking of saying no Natalie replied "I have never been to a horse race."

"That's settled then – the doctors will allow you out for the day with me."

"Oh Jeremy you are so good to me. Now I have something to look forward to."

What Jeremy didn't tell her was that he had had to fight to get the doctors to agree, and that he was not to over tire her. He had also promised to try and get her to eat a small healthy meal – he even had a diet list – and that she was to be back by 5 .30pm. Well, none of this was going to phase Lord Castle.

In the days since Natalie had been rushed into hospital she had had many hours to reflect upon her life. At first she was sure that Stefan would come into the hospital to see her. Slowly, however, the realisation came to her that he had never cared for her – and had simply used her as an easy money option. His erratic behaviour, late nights and uncommunicative moments all pointed to one possibility when combined with all the money he had needed –Stefan was a drug addict and she had been his bank.

Feeling somewhat nauseous as she had made a supreme effort to eat as much of the small meal which had been brought to her as she could. Natalie reflected on her recent conversation with Adrian Ravenscroft and Isobel Courtin. Her future was a dark uncertain path but at least she knew that it no longer included dance, Adrian had been kind as he closed the door.

"I'm sorry Natalie, but we have had to make a permanent re-placement of a new lead in your position. Unfortunately your doctors cannot give any indication of when you will be able to leave hospital, never mind work again."

Although she felt weak Natalie smiled bravely "Of course Adrian; you have all your commitments and the rest of the company to consider. I really do understand."

"There will always be a place for you in the chorus whenever you wish."

Natalie looked askew at Isobel as he said this.

Does he really think I would return as one of the chorus after being the principal?

To save further embarrassment Adrian and Isobel quickly left. Isobel hugged Natalie to herself briefly and whispered softly "If you ever need any help at all my dear, please do not hesitate to call me." It was to be many years before Natalie asked her mentor for help, but when it came it was invaluable.

Scared and uncertain Natalie knew she would have to draw deep into her inner mental reserves to get well. She had no real plan for doing this or indeed what she would do with the rest of her life- at just 23 she was now retired from dance. All her life dance had dominated her every waking moment. What would she do now? Well at least she still had the friendship of Jeremy and her father`s money. The anti depressant drugs they gave her caused mild hallucinations and as she drifted off to sleep she imagined her self in a wooded clearing dancing again, but the image was very hazy and unclear, *what was the large animal doing there with her? And was it a deer?*

By Friday Natalie was feeling a little better and was really looking forward to her day out. The arrangement was that Jeremy would pick her up early and take her back to her flat to change; then they would motor up to Cheltenham.

Nervous of how she looked and unsure of herself Natalie walked out of the hospital with Jeremy, the first surprise of many was when a Rolls Royce, a fancy coat of arms on the door, drew up at the kerb by them. The driver got out saluted, bowed to her and opened the door. Natalie had only met Jeremy a few times before and had no idea that he was rich and had a title.

Jeremy, realising that perhaps he should have filled her in a little about himself also felt nervous and self conscious as he reflected that in wanting Natalie to like him for himself and not his title or fortune he may have left out too much.

The day did not get off to a good start when they arrived at Natalie's flat to find Stefan had cleared out the flat leaving very little of anything. Natalie's belongings even most of her clothes had gone. She sat stunned on her bed surrounded by chaos, but not much else.

"I can't go like this!" she said tearfully. Natalie was wearing a dark track suit and Nike trainers.

"Let's go shopping then."

Natalie brightened somewhat. Then her face clouded over again.

Jeremy saw how careful he had to be it was all in her face, hurt, distrust, dependence, resentment of her own dependence and concern about money.

Jeremy was not only rich and titled, but also a very good lawyer and diplomat

"Why don't you go shopping then – I have an advance on your money here. I brought it in case you wanted to place a bet – but even better if you buy an outfit – then maybe you will permit me to place a bet for you."

"OK. Oxford Street, here I come."

Once she had made up her mind Natalie was impressively motivated and although Jeremy had resigned himself to being hours late within three quarters of an hour she was looking absolutely superb, if waif like, with an elegant cream outfit complete with hat and jacket new soft calf shoes with medium heels -to walk round the course, she told Jeremy and a matching bag –Jeremy handed her some money to pay. For a moment she hesitated, thinking of all the debts –but Jeremy smiled at her encouragingly and she quickly paid and walked out of the shop without looking back.

With so many wins under his belt over the last two years Running Winds odds in the week before the race were quite high and he was the favourite, but Kauto Star- last years winner was also on high odds. The occasional tantrums which Running Wind could throw kept his price lower than his talent merited. Twice last year he had simply planted his feet and refused to run. In the last two years Peter Lake had learnt not to change anything in Running Wind's schedule and certainly never to try another jockey; Freddy O'Hara's broken collar bone was proof of that. Running Wind had dumped him right at the start. This was it! The beginning of the new era; his solicitor had drawn up the contract and prospective share owners were lining up. As soon as Running Wind won the cup 40 new owners would have a share in him at £50 000 each. £2 million-- his fortune would be made by this wonder horse. The Triple Crown? The Grand National? Why not? –He knew this horse was capable.

So much had happened in the last few months that Natalie felt that life was almost surreal. As they drove Jeremy filled her in on the details of himself. He was actually Lord Castle – since his father's death a few years previously and although he worked in London, his family home was in Oxfordshire. His uncle was the estate manager and lived there with his family in the lodge while Jeremy's mother and two sisters lived in the large Elizabethan house." They will all be there today. We have a box."

Natalie was beginning to feel out of her depth, but Jeremy was such good company and he promised she would love his youngest sister Clare as she was a classical musician.

When they arrived in the car park at the race course Jeremy's car was allowed into the owner's park where the chauffeur left them at the gate.

The gateman obviously knew Jeremy and he tipped his hat to him and let them in, "Her ladyship is in the box, Sir."

Natalie drew back her shoulders as if she were going on stage. Determined not to be intimidated she took Jeremy's out stretched arm and walked calmly to meet his family.

They were nearly bowled over on the way by a collision with a whirlwind red headed 15 year old young girl, slim and freckled.

Laughing Jeremy introduced Clare, the promising young musician of the family.

Natalie need not have worried. As Clare quickly claimed her for her own and with her benign manipulation guided Natalie through all the polite greetings and introductions and then led Natalie off –ostensibly to place a bet, but in truth Clare really wanted to pick Natalie's brains about the musicians she had met in her Ballet career.

As Clare gushed on about different operas and asked Natalie about famous dancers and musicians, Natalie replied on the surface. Inside she reflected upon Jeremy and his family – his mother white haired and kind had obviously once been a great beauty. She had superb style and grace and although her manner was a little daunting, Natalie realised that this was her normal way and not a direct inflection on herself. Clare's sister Annabel was a little shallow for Natalie's taste. Seemingly interested only in what everyone was wearing or doing – in a sharp sometimes sarcastically funny, commentary for her mother Annabel missed nothing and her scathing tongue was far reaching. Although if one counted only outside appearances Annabel was a slim elegant and very pretty woman, but her snake like venomous comments and snide looks showed the depth of her callous character.

Natalie entertained Clare for some twenty minutes during which time she had yet to even see a horse closer than the tiny matchbox figures of the far distance.

Jeremy appeared just as Natalie was truly beginning to wish Clare elsewhere and announced to Clare that he had promised to take Natalie down to the collecting ring to see his horse.

Overhead the tannoy announced that the next race was indeed today's top race, the Cheltenham Gold Cup.

Jeremy's horse Duplex was a stunning looker a chestnut mare with a flaxen mane and tail. She really stood out from the plentiful browns and bays with only 2 greys and one other very dark chestnut gelding. At 20 to 1 she was obviously not the favourite –but Jeremy was not too bothered "She won the Champion Hurdle and winners of that race do not often win here – I have backed her to be placed."

Natalie showed confusion at all this.

"I hope she will come in second or third. Obviously I would love her to win, but I am a realist. However a good result is important as she goes to stud next year and the better she does this season the more her offspring will be worth."

"So do I bet on her?" Natalie asked him.

"Well, if you wish you can have a small tote bet each way on her."

Again Natalie frowned.

Laughing Jeremy explained that she would be betting that the horse would finish first, second or third then if she did Natalie would have a small gain, and he then said to be fair she should put a small flutter on her choice as this would make the race more exciting.

"I promised you the spending money." Jeremy finished, handing her a white envelope.

Before she could even protest or open the envelope Jeremy called to Clare who was walking by and told her to help Natalie make her bets.

When she got to the tote stands Natalie was shocked to discover £200 in ten pound notes in the envelope.

Clare was nonplussed when Natalie seemed embarrassed by the money

"Oh that's pocket money to Jer;" Clare reassured her. "Right which horse?"

Natalie remembered while they waited to see Duplex led out seeing the favourite a coppery bay with a white blaze and left hind white sock. He had been prancing and dancing at the end of the lead rope held by an elderly man.

"The favourite!" she replied.

"Oh yes Running Wind. He's a real character. They sometimes have trouble with him going up to the start. Right then what's it to be?"

Natalie felt like she was the younger girl as Clare took charge.

She took £100 of Natalie's cash and put a bet on to win for Running Wind.

Then put the other £50 on Duplex each way.

She then added a £50 bet her own idea on Kuato Star the 2007 winner.

Natalie was indeed glad Clare had been with her. Even though it was not her money, she would never have found the courage to put so much on the outcome of a horse race on her own.

The excitement was building and Natalie felt the atmosphere charged like it was just before the curtain rose on a first night. She was beginning to understand why so many people were drawn to horse racing.

The fate of her money was on the speed and power of a four legged elegant running machine.

Clare led her down onto the rails where Jeremy was waiting. The whole bet laying exercise was obviously set up but Natalie was grateful for Jeremy's thoughtfulness in this as she knew that with him she would never have been able to bet his money. Clare had made it seem easy and right.

"Just in time," he said.

On the overhead screens they could see the horses being led to the start.

Suddenly, a horse started to play up on the screen they could easily see that it was the bay Running Wind.

"God, he's at it again!" Clare exclaimed "He should keep his energy for the race."

"But. What a horse!" Jeremy said with admiration as Running Wind reared and spun. "They say most jockeys refuse to ride him, but Rob Steel says he's just misunderstood and has superb talent."

Finally with all the horses including the favourite, in line at the post, the race got underway. On the overhead screens they could see the mud flying as the horses cleared the first of the 22 fences.

At the second fence two horses came down and now one was running still with no rider aboard.

The next mile was uneventful but as they drew near to where Jeremy, Natalie and Clare were standing they could see Running Wind speeding up as he ran the long way round all the other horses. He passed most of them easily and soared over the fence landing so beautifully he looked set to win the race. Duplex was just behind him in second place with Kuato Star neck and neck with the favourite.

Just as they were level with Natalie they took off for the ditch fence and the horse beside Running Wind took off badly, as if trying to take up the fence by the roots and lurched sideways into Running Wind. Horrified Natalie watched in slow motion as Running Wind stumbled and launched Rob Steel over his head. He staggered for a few steps then fell rolling over. As Rob got to his feet the horse lay motionless.

The other horses ran on and everyone's attention was drawn to the race –but Natalie who had never been to a horse race before could not take her eyes off the scene in front of her. The horse had now raised his head and was trying to struggle to his feet. He pushed up with a huge grunt but held one of his front legs up; he appeared unable to bare any weight on this leg.

A horse ambulance with a vet on board rolled up as the flying mud from the horses was still settling.

A temporary screen was erected around the horse so Natalie slowly crept closer so she could see between the sides of the screen.

Irate voices came from inside.

"How much?"

"I do not know exactly. It's a new treatment that I've heard about."

"This bloody horse has just lost me thousands of pounds and you want me to spend more!"

"Well he's insured isn't he?" Bill insisted. After all it was only last month he had reminded Peter to up the insurance policy on Running Wind.

Not meeting Bills gaze Peter said heavily –"No! I never renewed."

Rob Steel the jockey appeared on the scene having been given the all clear from the course doctor. He entered the screened area.

Looking fondly at Running Wind he asked Bill how the horse was.

"Not properly insured that's what he is." Bill said bitterly.

"What!"-- Rob glared at Peter.

"Put him down Ian-"- Peter said heavily to the course vet.

"NO!!!! " A cry came from behind the screen.

Natalie, unaware of race course etiquette, was now standing inside the screen.

"He`s my bloody horse. I'll do what I like with him." Peter glared at this overwrought young woman as she stood before him shaking.

Through her tears Natalie screamed at him. "Sell him to me then instead."

The scene seemed unreal and Natalie was taken for a hysterical do gooder

Only Rob wanted to take her seriously and was glad as he had tremendous respect for Running Wind and would not have wanted to see him destroyed.

No one else would have given Natalie's wishes any credence but Jeremy arrived just at that point. The race was over and Duplex had come fourth, the winner was Kuato Star.

The arrival of the well known Lord Castle changed things.

"What is going on here!" he cried gently drawing Natalie to himself.

Rob spoke first and filled Jeremy in.

"Running Wind came down and has injured his left superficial digital flexor tendon. Normally a horse will never race again after such an injury, but there is a new treatment. A company in Canterbury called Tendon Works have developed the treatment, but it takes at least 10 weeks and is costly Peter has informed us that the horse is not insured and he want's to euthanize him."

"I will buy him and pay for his treatment" Natalie cried. She was so upset she was barely aware of what she was saying.

"Are you sure?" Jeremy asked her.

"Yes…. he is damaged; like me…we can…we can…. heal together."

This one small statement convinced Jeremy. He had been increasingly worried about Natalie and how she was going to cope when the full impact of not ever dancing again hit her. At least this would be an all encompassing project for her; after all he knew she could afford it.

He took Peter Lake apart from the group.

"Will you take my personal cheque until we can sort this out?"

Lord Castle was known as the most honest man on the race circuit.

"Yes of course," Peter replied gruffly. This really was surreal.

"How much?" reaching into his inside jacket pocket Jeremy withdrew his cheque book.

Peter was aware that with Jeremy, Bill, Ian and Rob not to mention three race course officials present that the price would have to be fair and reflect the situation Peter had just lost £10,000 on top of any future winnings from Running Wind which could have been considerable, and the syndicate money. However, there was not much chance of the horse returning to racing and as a gelding he was no use for breeding. He took a chance at a high demand £10,000. If he could get back his betting money he could at least still keep on training- but the fire in him had died as Running Wind fell.

Jeremy knew it was much more than the horse was worth but one look at Natalie's pleading eyes and he wrote out the cheque, signing it with a flourish and handing it to Peter. Grabbing the cheque Peter Lake ordered Bill to come with him and left abruptly, chased by one of the race course officials who wanted more information.

Bill's look of agonised concern and sadness as he left was hauntingly imprinted in Natalie's mind. Behind the screen however Jeremy's influence was paramount and it was quickly arranged that Running Wind would be stabled overnight at the course. A stale-mate situation was prevented when Rob Steel forwarded the information that his sister ran a dressage yard near Newmarket and that Running Wind could be taken there tomorrow.

Jeremy was thankful how easily it was all arranged as he still had to get Natalie back to the hospital as quickly as possible. Fortunately Clare offered to come with Jeremy and she sat with Natalie and talked ballet, music and horses all the way home, brilliantly defusing any tensions there may have been.

A lovely horse is always an experience; it is an emotional experience of the kind which is spoiled by words.
Beryl Markaham

Chapter 6

The next day Rob called David Chapman –Jones of Tendon Works about Running Wind. David asked several questions and then explained to Rob that as the horse had been injured only 8 days ago it could be some time before he could be moved; however he was willing to come the next day to examine and assess Running Wind.

David arrived very punctually which he admitted was unusual for him and as he stepped from his car Rob had a sense that all would be well now – he exuded calm and confidence – even the sometimes difficult to handle Running Wind was relaxed when David examined him. Rob had, after speaking with David on the phone expected an older man, but was supremely assured by this tall, blonde and very athletic man; the fitness and dedication David so very obviously had, reassured the jockey in Rob.

"He has badly damaged his left digital flexor tendon –it will be at least three weeks before he will be fit enough to travel."

Quite lame Running Wind was obviously in a lot of pain. Sue had arranged for her local vet to be there as discussions were held on pain relieving medication and on the subject of box rest. It was arranged that David would return to transport Running Wind to his yard in about one month's time when the surrounding inflammation round the tendon had had time to settle down.

Natalie looked up, as a man approached-- since that fateful Friday she had not had any real visitors, only the hospital staff and doctors. This man was vaguely familiar to her.

Striding up to her bed the slight, small but handsome man met her gaze confidently and held out his hand to her.

"I was the jockey riding Running Wind when he fell!" He announced. "Your horse is stabled at my sister's yard now. I came to tell you he is fine, settled in and as comfortable as he can be."

"Thank you so very much." Natalie truly was grateful to this man –she could remember every minute of the fiasco at the races and was a little at a loss as to what to do next.

Rob sensed this and made it easy for her. "I hope you don't mind, but I have taken the liberty of contacting David Chapman-Jones on your behalf. "

Natalie looked confused so Rob quickly continued.

"Sorry. David is the man who devised the tendon treatment we hope will heal Running Wind. He has spoken with my sister's vet and would like the horse in his stables in a few weeks. I understand that it would be difficult for you to do much from in here." He looked round her hospital room." But I can arrange it all if you would like. I rode Running Wind in many races and we won most of them. I…well….I have great respect for the old boy." He finished reluctant to show too much emotion.

"I would appreciate your help. I don't even know your name."

"Rob Steel –I know yours. Natalie." He said wryly. "It's on the board at the bottom of your bed!"

Natalie stood transfixed as a very sedated Running Wind was slowly backed out of the horse box. She was very impressed by David Chapman –Jones and his team as they gently and with great patience led her horse to a large stable which was light and airy. There was an attached area with wood fibre floor of about 240sq feet. "Running Wind will be able to walk out into this area when he likes during the day." David reassured Natalie. This surprised her as Sue`s vet had said the only possible way the horse could recover was for him to be as confined as possible. She voiced her doubts.

"I have this all the time "David sighed. "Despite all my success with my methods the old school vets do not want to listen or believe me."

Natalie thought he looked saddened for the first time and realised he took this criticism personally.

David then explained to Rob and Natalie that Running Wind had sustained a great deal of damage to his tendon in the fall. "The spaghetti like strands which make up the tendon are seriously enlarged and fluid has built up. We will be scanning his leg to find the exact location of the tissue damage to the superficial flexor-tendon, because the swelling has pushed the deep digital tendon sideways." He paused to make sure Natalie was taking it all in. "My vet, Archie Mc Pherson, will prescribe a course of pain relieving medication and we will fit a cast to the back of his lower leg." Seeing Natalie's alarm at this David added quickly "Don't worry he will be able to walk with this in place and his other leg will also be supported. Treatment with Cyro therapy use of extreme cold; to reduce the swelling caused by the journey will be followed by the Synapse patented cell regeneration process. Although it is some-what uncomfortable it will encourage rapid cell regeneration."

Avril Wilson

Natalie did not fully understand all the treatments David explained, but she felt in her heart that she really was doing the right thing. Most importantly David had been very positive and reassuring about Running Wind's chances of full recovery. "He has a strong and determined personality which will help him immensely with his recovery."

Rob was impressed by David Chapman Jones, and his team in Canterbury enthusiastic and obviously very competent. The welfare and treatment of each horse was under his personal supervision and he truly wanted all the horses to profit from his radical treatment and have a new chance in life. Natalie was particularly moved to think that Running Wind would make a full recovery as she knew if she had not so precipitately interfered, then Running Wind would already be dead. Somehow just thinking of this helped her to get through the days which had seemingly become longer and longer recently; she decided to focus on two things- Running Wind's health and of course her own.

It was arranged that Rob and Natalie would visit Running Wind every week to check on his progress.

It seemed to Natalie that her horse was improving every week although David explained that it was actually a delicate balance and that the struggle to keep the skin of the horse's leg in good condition while he was in a plaster cast was very difficult and involved often very expensive but effective dressings. Natalie began to understand why this treatment was not cheap. At first Natalie looked upon this beautiful equine as if he belonged to someone else, but slowly she began to feel genuine love for this horse, although she was in awe of his size and even though he was in pain, power. Sometimes – though she would never have admitted it to any one, she had an inner imagination vision of

87

herself riding this beautiful horse. All seemed to be going well with his recovery.

The sky was black and threatening, dark clouds scudding along and the wind beginning to lift leaves and straw wisps from the ground. When David had seen the weather forecast last night his first thought was of the North wing of the stable block. The roof was due for strengthening work the following week as David felt that the overhanging branches of nearby trees were a real danger and the builders had already delivered materials on site. *Damn that jumped up little jobs worth from the council! If he hadn't slapped that protection order on those trees I could have removed those two old Walnuts. He wouldn't have it that they are rotten inside. Six months of administrative red tape later and countless letters to the council and still no permission to remove even a twig!* Containing his anger with difficulty he and his team were rushing around the yard attaching things, tying down anything likely to move and generally keeping watch on all the horses and their reactions to the storm.

A loud clap of thunder rent the air, followed a few seconds later by a blinding flash. Counting the gap between the thunder and lightning David realised the storm was very close. The next flash illuminated the sky for a split second and huge rain drops began to cascade down on the running men.

Picking up momentum the wind seemed to be screaming its wrath and started lifting anything in its path The two gnarled old Walnut trees were creaking and groaning. Their branches, dangerously heavy with green fruits, were waving and swaying. Small twigs with Walnuts attached broke off almost like throwing little warnings.

A massive crash sounded by the North side of the stables! Dreading the worst David and Pete ran without thinking into the shaking building, each grabbing a head collar from the hooks by the door.

Flashes of lightning could now be seen through the roof. "God!" thought David steeling himself for what he might see. He could hear the equine squeals as he ran. Most of the stables were un-touched, only two had horses in them Pete quickly led Summertime out of her stable and into the yard. Right at the back was Running Wind's large stable. David ran on horrified to see the roof had collapsed right over this last stable.

In the corner cowed, the horse was hardly visible beneath what looked like a whole tree. Running Wind was shaking and trying to rise; his squeals could be heard far into the yard.

"Go and phone the vet! " David cried as Pete returned. David then made what most people would consider a suicidal move and entered the stable – a huge branch had ripped free from the tree of its life and crashed through the roof landing on the horse. David could hardly bear to look. The massive branch had hit his good front leg, and was pinning him down. As David approached Running Wind he whickered to him --- "Yes, I know boy –just stay still let me get this thing off you." Although years of working with horses had left little room for David to be amazed at their behaviour; Running Wind's obvious compre-hension of the situation was still startling – the huge terrified beast lay quiet while David tried to break away the branch but it was too heavy. He could see that the remainder of the roof was close to collapse. He knelt by the horse to examine the damage. Scattered green Walnuts laying witness to the trees origins were all over the stable floor. Fury against the local council rose again in David.

"Is it bad?"... a voice came from behind him ....Archie was suddenly there.

"We have to get this great lump of tree off him first. I can't really see but it has fallen mostly on his good leg. "

Archie took a syringe from his bag and filled it with tranquilizer David put out his hand for the syringe. There was no space for the vet to get near enough. David quickly inserted the needle and emptied the contents into the neck of the horse.

Pete had returned with a 2 bow saws and an axe, the three men cut at the smaller branches. The wind was still howling and shouts and crashes could be heard from the yard. The timbers holding up the remainder of the roof creaked and a shower of tiles fell into the next stall. The horse was nearly free as they struggled to lift the tree. He rolled his terrified eyes, the whites showing real fear. He started tossing his head until David fixed him with a gaze. "Steady boy…its fine….good"As he spoke he stroked the mane and neck of the panicked horse. Archie was impressed how calm and soothing David's voice was as he was in a very vulnerable position. Finally the branch came away and Archie and Pete carried it out. David watched Running Wind as he rose to his knees with effort, reluctant now to put weight on either leg. The tranquilizer had kicked in and the horse's expression was subdued almost peaceful. David ran his hand slowly and carefully down each front leg. He took a great gulp of air when he confirmed no breaks, only then realising how long he had been holding his breath. Archie returned and the two men carefully helped Running Wind to his feet. With haste they then tried to lead the injured horse out. Drugged with tranquilizer he dragged his hind legs and staggered, as a further huge gust threatened the rest of the roof. Slowly they led Running Wind drunkenly out into the yard. The rain was heavy now, sheets of it moving like ghosts seen in glimpses in the lightning flashes and back lit by the yard lights.

Relief flooded through David.

Archie bent over to examine the horse. He gave Running Wind an anti biotic and anti inflammatory injection. "Well as it is his good leg it could be worse, but it will have its own repercussions."

Natalie was shocked – she had just put down the phone to David. Glad though she was that her horse had survived the trauma of the storm she was seriously concerned what would happen with his treatment now he had seriously injured his good leg. How could he even put weight on it never mind get the exercise which would prevent the muscles atrophying?

Arriving later at the yard to see Running Wind, Natalie felt quite annoyed as she found David was actually out. "He has gone to the accident and emergency unit of the local hospital to fetch some-thing. He asked me to tell you to wait, he has something to show you" His assistant explained.

Natalie was standing talking with Running Wind in a large brick barn safe from the weather. She was stroking his nose when David returned. He was carrying two large sealed polythene bags inside which were a clear and orange plastic tube.

"Hello Natalie… don`t worry about your horse. I have an idea! As you know he needs to keep some mobility and this new injury is a problem, but this should help." He held up the bag.

"What is that you have there? " Natalie questioned, still slightly cross that David wasn't by Running Wind's side.

"I have used one of these before. It is a Pneumatic Polymer splint or in layman's terms an inflatable leg support of the type used in road traffic accidents to immobilise limbs. If it is not inflated to a very high pressure it should help support Running Wind's leg and allow him to put some weight on it and thus exercise. Brilliant even if I say so myself! Not exactly conventional practice but doing things by the book has never really been my style and I think it will work."

Filled with gratitude for this clever man and rather guilty for her earlier cross feelings towards David who, she appreciated was wholly responsible for her horse's healing programme, Natalie un-characteristically gave David a long hug and a kiss on his cheek.

"Have you ever seen anything like that? "David laughed as he finished putting the splints on, Running Wind's new leggings looked like inflated long socks. With relief Natalie allowed herself to relax giggling she agreed she had never seen anything like it, and she gave David's hand a grateful squeeze. David took a photo of Running Wind commenting, "Not one for the Racing Post just yet, I do not think the veterinary world is ready for this one!"

Treatment was then continued with the plaster cast, and the other leg supported by the inflatable splint and a bandage.

Finally the swelling caused by the falling branch was reduced and the leg was recovering well. Walking on a treadmill for a few minutes once, then twice a day, was the next treatment and after only a week an improvement was observed.

 Bandaging and pain relievers were used when it was felt they were needed. Although sometimes uncomfortable for the horse the synapse cell regeneration treatment was continued and the treatment checked by ultrasound examinations.

Care was always taken to insure that no sudden movement put stress on the tendons and therefore undo the recovery work.

Four months later Rob and Natalie arrived early to see Running Wind walking on the treadmill for a longer session; David met them with a smile. "The tendons much more closely resemble normal ones."

Natalie was delighted; finally she could relax and truly believe her horse was healing.

Ironically involving herself in this horse and his treatment was very therapeutic and beneficial to Natalie, although she was seeing the hospital psychiatric doctor on a regular basis – rest and occupation with Running Wind were to prove to be the best medicine. It seemed Natalie was more concerned about the welfare of this horse than herself. Her strength began to return and she found herself much more interested in eating on days when she was to go and visit her horse. Sometimes however the enormity of what she had done, not just rescuing Running Wind but in becoming involved in a horse and his welfare almost over-whelmed her with concerns about this responsibility. Although she would not even admit it, inwardly she was more than a bit scared. It made her, however, look closely at her own life and as her horse regained his strength so too did Natalie. Far reaching thoughts still came to Natalie of Stefan and his total betrayal – it would be a long time before Natalie would be prepared to give her heart to a man but for the moment it was her growing love for Running Wind which truly sustained her.

Driving to David's yard, Natalie was feeling somewhat low and nervous; this was the first time she had driven on her own since her collapse. When Rob had phoned last night and explained that he had fallen from a horse and broken his ankle she had at first decided not to make the weekly trip alone. Later the depth of her disappointment surprised her and made her change her mind. As it turned out David was also very busy –but his suggestion to Natalie was that she could go and see Running Wind in his stable. One of the grooms took Natalie to the stable and left her. Her horse had his back to her and was apparently asleep his left hind leg cocked. The stress of driving herself now coupled with neither Rob nor David being with her and her horse not even noticing her caused her some distress and she sank down onto a straw bale next to the stable. As she sat down Running Wind woke up and put his head out to see who was there and connect with them. Natalie looked up and smiled, to pass the time she started to talk to him - at first in a rambling way, but as she sensed the animal's interest she began to tell him the story of her life. She spoke with complete honesty and openness in a way she would never have done with any of the doctors she saw daily at the hospital. Running Wind kept his head out of his stable and turned towards Natalie, as she spoke slowly he lowered his head and touched Natalie's shoulder. She kept speaking until she had literally given the horse her life history. They remained in silence together for a long time afterwards, the horse still touching Natalie gently with his nose, until David found them. Although he did not know exactly what had occurred between the horse and Natalie, David sensed that their relationship had deepened. Natalie had seen for the first time just how spiritual a being a horse is.

The improvement in Natalie was quickly noticed by the doctors at the hospital. The supervising Psychiatrist called into the office of the physician dealing with Natalie a couple of days later.

"Well, who has tapped into Miss Diaz and cleared her head?" He asked.

Jennifer Swann shook her own head –"We are as amazed as you are," she confessed. "She went out on her own to visit this stable she goes to and almost the moment she came back we saw a change- a real shift in her behaviour. I truly believe she will be able to leave here soon now."

Dr Noble then called Natalie into his office.

"Miss Diaz, may I congratulate you on your improvement and ask how this remarkable change has come about."

With a wry smile Natalie replied with utter truthfulness "I told someone who understood everything."

Supremely interested the doctor leaned towards Natalie and asked, "Who?"

"Running Wind, of course." Natalie seemed surprised to be asked.

At first the doctor thought he was becoming the butt of a joke, but Natalie continued. "My horse-I see him every week. He is recovering just like me."

Normally lots of people are there, only this time we were alone and I just started talking to him. Before I knew it I had told him the whole story. I guess I did not realise how much pressure my parents had always put on me to achieve in ballet, but I felt such sympathy from Running Wind. He must have had a similar life as a talented race horse he was always expected to full fill the expectations of others."

Still unconvinced exactly who had really helped Natalie, only sure that she was on the road to recovery, the doctors agreed that it was time for her to leave.

As her horse was going to be stabled in Newmarket after his treatment by David, Natalie decided to move there when she finally left the hospital.

Nearly a month in hospital had left Natalie more than a little insecure and not knowing Newmarket or anyone there apart from Rob she was grateful when he offered to help her find a house. Talking with Jeremy about her finances he had suggested that she buy a cottage rather than rent one as property prices were riseing and a two bedroomed cottage was always a good investment in Newmarket. Natalie decided to invest nearly half of her inheritance and Rob had scoured several estate agencies and arranged viewings of four properties. Natalie found the first two over modernised and the third too close to a noisy road. The fourth cottage they visited was in a quiet cul de sac and backed on to open fields –in front it opened directly onto the road but behind it had a lovely, large garden as it was an end of terrace and thus had a triangular garden with some mature trees and a lawn bordered by flowers. The estate agent informed them in her brisk, pinstriped suited, efficient way that the current owners were keen gardeners. Natalie felt a deep sense of peace in this garden surrounded by the fragrant multi coloured flowers and loved the views of open fields. Inside the house was far from perfect, being too cluttered and twee, but Natalie knew that stripped of the overbearing furniture and knickknacks...and painted white, the charm of the old beams Pammet tiles and fireplace would make up for the size. It had a small kitchen leading to a much larger living room with the fireplace. "The Jotul wood burning stove is staying," the agent pointed out – realising Natalie's interest and working hard to earn her commission. Upstairs there were two bedrooms, one a good size and the other small but big enough for a double bed and a shower room which had obviously been recently redecorated. Never one to hesitate in life Natalie decided on the spot to buy the cottage and as a first time buyer, with the sellers moving to Marbella in Spain, the purchase went through quickly and easily.

The months which followed were busy for Natalie. When she was not clearing, painting and gardening at 3 Church Row, she was making the journey to Canterbury to see how Running Wind was progressing with his treatment.

Having never seen a horse being shod before Natalie watched fascinated as the hot metal touched the hoof. Smoke filled the air and a heady scorched smell made Natalie's nostrils twitch. David introduced the farrier to Natalie and she could tell he was being genuine when he said, "I couldn't possibly do this work on the horses without Steve's help." He complimented the farrier. "He knows his stuff. There are very few I would trust with this and very few take the importance of correct shoeing seriously enough. We must make sure any lateral imbalance will be corrected and as much as possible ensure stress is taken off the digital flexor tendons."

When the shoeing was completed, Running Wind was walked out in hand for a few minutes for the first time. Natalie was charmed to see his desire for the grass as he snatched quick mouthfuls-- as if he was not sure how long he would be able to enjoy this delicacy.

"Soon he will be turned out in a 10 meter pen for up to an hour a day to eat grass." As David said this Natalie realised her horse was indeed healing fast and would soon be her whole responsibility.

Request often, be content with little, reward
lavishly.
*Francoise Baucher (A new method of Horse-
manship 1843)*

Chapter 7

The heady almost childish excitement Natalie had felt when
Running Wind stepped out of the trailer and raised his head
and whinnied in Sue's yard, had slowly given way to worried
concerns about handling this huge equine. At first Running
Wind was easy to lead out of his stable, the horse was quiet and
a little subdued. Even the inexperienced Natalie could lead him.
After a few days however Running Wind's true character re
emerged. Natalie was finding it increasingly difficult to cope
with just putting on the head collar and leading Running Wind
to the pasture. The other day she had failed with Running Wind
turning away and raising his head and had had to ask one of
the lads to help her. Jim Style had taken the head collar and,
shouting at the horse had gone up to him and given him a hefty
kick in the ribs then roughly shoved the head collar on and
dragged him out. As he handed the rope to Natalie he said –
"Just needs telling whose boss is all."

Shaken by this demonstration of aggressive bullying Natalie was depressed. She wanted to learn how to control the big equine that she loved, but not like this!

When Rob next came to visit Natalie broached the subject with him, as a Jockey she expected Rob to side with the lads who all thought she was too soft with her horse.

"Has Running Wind been out today yet? "

Natalie shook her head and with shame admitted that she had been unable to take him to the pasture for three days.

"The lads do it for me –but I can't watch."

Rob led the way to Running Wind's stable. Taking the head collar which hung by the door he slowly and softly entered the stable. As the horse turned towards him he stood completely still holding out his hand for him to sniff. He then gently started to caress Running Wind all over his body with soft circular strokes as if he had all day. Rob just stood quietly next to the horse and rubbed his nose, legs and flanks. Finally, with a sigh Running Wind dropped his head near Rob, the jockey then gently put on the halter pulling the horses head over to himself with a soft flexion.

He then stood at the horse's shoulder and tapped him on his back until he took a few steps towards the door, Running Wind then walked quietly to his paddock and when Rob released him he did not head off as usual but remained near Rob who caressed him again.

Natalie watched all this quietly amazed. It had taken Rob nearly half an hour to lead Running Wind out but he was a calm and much happier horse she wanted to know how to do it.

"Oh Rob this is how I want to be with Running Wind."

"That's what I came to tell you, I've been watching a lot about how these Natural Horsemanship people work and it really is so impressive. Rob knew that Melanie would take this horse back into her care and that she –with Bills help, could rehabilitate him. However Bill had vanished. Rob had not seen him since he walked off the race course with Peter Lake. He had to find a solution for Natalie or there could be real trouble and danger for her. "Two of them are coming to Newmarket next month to hold a clinic for two days. Shane and Meredith Ransley from Australia and they are looking for a horse to break as a demonstration. They call it colt starting, and I thought of Running Wind."

"But he is already broken, he has run in races!"

"Yes, but they will re start horses and I talked with David about his leg. He says that he is ready for some work."

"I can show you a few basic things to do with him, and then Shane will retrain him. It will make it so much easier for you when you do decide to ride him."

Natalie stared at Rob--- she had never spoken to anyone -- even Rob of her inner desire to ride her horse.

"He's too much for me!" she dismissed the idea, "I cannot even ride."

"That's the other thing, I talked with Sue and she would like to give you some riding lessons if you will teach her youngest daughter to dance. She hates riding, unlike her sister, but really wants to dance."

It all seemed to happen so quickly. Natalie sent an email to Meredith at the address Rob gave her... which he had found on the internet. The team were called` Quantum Savvy'. Meredith replied with friendly and positive advice about handling Running Wind, confirming that they would use him in their demonstration, and that Natalie could then watch the weekend clinic.

Ellie had an instinctive feel for music. She reminded Natalie so much of herself at the same age she knew as soon as she saw her dance that not only could she help this child, but that she really wanted to. At 13 Ellie was slim, lithe and very supple if a little too tall. Although she lacked the control which comes from hours of balance and point training, she had a superb sense of natural rhythm. Natalie knew that it was really, nearly too late for Ellie to train as a classical ballerina but recent years had seen taller ballerinas and much more interest in professional dancers for the stage and screen. Secretly Natalie hoped that Ellie would choose a career in this discipline and not as a classical ballerina – she knew Sue and her husband Tom would support Ellie whatever – The Mobley's were a true horse family –who, as owners of a dressage yard lived, ate and breathed horses, but they were not blind to the fact that their youngest daughter was more interested in dancing than riding. Natalie had taken to Sue. Taller by a couple of inches than her brother she wore her reddish blond hair tied back in a practical pigtail. Natalie was to learn that nearly every thing about Sue was immensely practical. From her no nonsense approach to the horses in her yard, to her dedication and warm encouraging ways with her dressage pupils. A superb cook and good mother to her three daughters only one of whom, Ellie, remained at home, she was a great all rounder.

It seemed to be a parallel learning curve as Ellie worked hard and improved upon her natural talent in ballet, so Natalie worked hard using her supreme sense of balance and suppleness to learn to ride. Natalie, teaching for the first time, had never even had a pupil before; she saw some exceptional talent shining through. Sue, who had had many pupils, had never met one with Natalie's sense of determination, balance and commitment to sheer hard work before. She was charmed.

Natalie worked Ellie almost as hard as she worked herself. Despite her young age Ellie felt she had to prove herself even more to her family because she was not riding horses and such was determined to do well. Natalie was the perfect teacher. She had been through it all herself and in a strange conspiratorially way the two exchanged notes. Natalie started to really do well as a rider. In a true twist to the tale the horse Natalie learnt to ride on had, ironically been bought for Ellie. Ellie did indeed love her 16.2hh German Warm blood mare Roxy. She was a large but gentle horse and was like a mountain for Natalie to get on. Sue had seldom seen so supple a pupil as she found in Natalie. She could easily vault onto Roxy, but after watching several pod cast videos on Shane and Meredith's web site she realised that she should mount slowly and with consideration for the horse. Sue was enchanted as Natalie jumped up and down next to Roxy then slowly mounted the big horse with agile ease, standing in the stirrup as if asking Roxy permission to be there.

"Right, Natalie, this week we are going to try the canter for the first time." Sue announced. Sue had been very impressed by Natalie's progress as she managed to master quickly from just walking Roxy to trotting, picking up the pace and beat of the rise to the trot very easily. "I want you to just trot slowly round in a quiet sitting trot. Make sure you do not tip forwards and place your inside leg on the girth and outside leg behind the girth as you ask Roxy for the upwards transition." Although she half expected the usual unbalanced lack of control and the possibility of a fall if Roxy lurched forward, she was therefore amazed as she watched Natalie canter slowly round the arena with superb balance and seemingly no fear for her first attempt. Natalie did confess to having a few butterflies just before the canter but the sensation of "flying" with her horse carried her away and she lost all sensation of fear. "It's so much more comfortable than the trot." Natalie was evidently thrilled. Sue knew that Roxy had a very even stride and was like sitting in an armchair at the canter. She was the perfect school master for Natalie. Food orientated and inclined to be lazy there was very little danger of her taking off too fast round the school and Sue watched her pupil gaining confidence each week. No one can learn to ride in just a few days….it takes weeks, months, even years of work, but Natalie was no stranger to hard work. Her innate sense of equilibrium meant that on the rare occasions when she lost her balance she nearly always landed on her feet. In ballet training, especially for the point work pain is commonplace and Natalie was very used to this. Her sheer joy in being in the saddle and naturally relaxed style really helped her to excel in this new discipline.

Some months later a friend of Sue's asked Natalie if she would teach her niece ballet. Word seemed to spread quickly and soon Natalie was teaching two afternoons and three evenings a week. This she was delighted about because she was now covering most of her living expenses. The money for Running Wind's treatment and paying off the debts Stefan had run up had all had to come out of her parent's money so she was eager not to keep using her savings.

The Quantum Savvy weekend was a massive turning point for Natalie. Rob had arranged transport for Running Wind to the event venue at a very well known yard and Natalie was there to help him when the horse arrived. Unfortunately he tensed coming out of the wagon into daylight and clattered awkwardly down the ramp. This caused a panic stricken moment where he cut his hock on the side of the ramp. The claustrophobic feeling inside a metal cage and anxiety at being separated from other horses had been too much for the insecure Running Wind. As a final show on arrival he reared fully, pulling up and back. Natalie was sure that if Rob had not been there he would have ended up totally un controllable. Rob approached the strung-up horse and with brave calm took his rope and led him forward, caressing and talking to him in a low voice.

Comments such as "Have you seen the wild race horse?" and "No one could ride that one!" were running in Natalie's ears – she was suffering nerves and serious doubts – *what if they were right and Running Wind threw Shane – what would she do next?*

The seating round the arena was completely full and as country music picked up the beat and a spot light lit the entrance a horse was led into the arena by Rob. He walked in a few paces and stopped. As arranged the spotlight then fell on a cowboy in a large Australian hat and Shane introduced himself and explained about Quantum Savvy. The Natural way to train and ride horses – Shane had studied with many of the worlds leading Natural Horsemanship trainers including Pat Parelli and was an expert in his field. In Australia Shane and Meredith had used their Quantum Savvy techniques, to rehabilitate many race horses.

Shane took the nervous Running Wind from Rob – then he just stood with him for some minutes as he explained to the audience what he was about to do. Visibly the horse started to relax. Before Rob left the arena he exchanged the conventional head collar for a string halter and 12' line.

As Shane turned to him, the horse lurched forward ....speaking into his small attached mike Shane kept the audience informed what he was doing.

"He is coming into my personal space," Shane said as he waved his arms in the air to block the horse, which then retreated back from him. "I need to earn his respect and trust and show him I want to keep him out of my personal space."

Quietly, a small wiry man crept to a ring side seat. He looked at no one and moved as if he did not wish to be seen or acknowledged. His curiosity had brought him here against his own skepticism and caution.

Bill watched transfixed as the spot light fell on the horse – *God!! It was indeed him......* As Shane sent the horse back by placing his hand on his chest the horse reared and as he rose he squealed. Shane then waved his stick towards the horse's nose to keep Running Wind out of his space again. Tears were in Bills eyes as he continued to watch and listen. Someone had told him that Running Wind was going to be the star attraction at this show but he had refused to believe them. As he watched he saw it was indeed the horse who had impressed Bill more than any other horse in his whole life. While the rest of the audience was oohing and ahhing at Running Wind as he reared, Bill was moved to see a horse that everyone, except two slim young women, had written off as useless. Melanie had won his trust way back and found her way forward with him. His career had then been put back on track. However life had let him down again and swamped his soul in pain through that horrendous injury and at no fault of his own. He had had such a bitter sweet life that Running Wind struggled to forgive pain and landed the blame firmly back on man. This evening now he was very obviously back on form – and true to form Bill thought wryly – *no one will just back this horse easily* – but Bill had reckoned without Shane and his Quantum Savvy ways.

"That's what he does to me," Natalie whispered to Rob "He pushes into me and knocks me backwards."

Smiling, Rob urged her to concentrate on Shane and the demonstration.

Shane caressed Running Wind with his horseman's stick... a long, plastic, non flexible kind of horse whip with a leather loop at the end to which was attached a long thin rope. Running Wind was afraid of this, remembering many times being struck by a whip, but even when he moved around and danced away Shane continued moving the stick...flicking the string without stopping whatever the horse did. Shane seemed to understand

Running Wind's fear and moved with him when he reacted, quietly persisting with swinging the string until the horse began to relax. Finally Shane could by using rhythmic strokes flick the line all over Running Wind and the horse remained calm. Shane then produced a longer line about 22' long and one inch thick, again with a leather end. Shane began passing this rope all over the horse. He reacted less to this than the first stick and soon would accept Shane throwing the rope over his flanks and back around his haunch, under his belly and round his legs.

Shane kept up a running commentary about what he was doing and why.

"Here I am de-sensitising the horse to the rope, string and stick. Even though Running Wind is an ex race horse and has been ridden in races, he has been in convalescence for over a year and if someone did try to ride him his only thought would be to run forward fast." As he spoke Shane was making Running Wind yield his hind quarters. A small jump had been set up and using the end of the rope to encourage him Shane sent the horse over the jump, asked him to yield his hind quarters then sent him back the other way.

"We have to control this forward motion while giving the horse confidence and building up his trust in us." He explained.

Shane then passed the rope round Running Winds middle exactly where the saddle sits. At first the horse was upset by the rope remembering the feel of a saddle and what it meant. The highly strung and sensitive Running Wind was backing up and rearing at the end of the rope. The audience in general and Natalie in particular, were seriously beginning to doubt whether Shane could really ride this wild horse. Quickly realising how sensitive to this Running Wind was Shane un-linked the rope and simply left the rope lying across the horses back. After a while Running Wind calmed down and as soon as he was happier Shane then passed the rope round his girth area again. He then tightened the rope a little and the horse set off running in a circle round Shane...when he slowed down and stopped moving Shane released the small amount of pressure he had put on.

"It is the release which teaches the horse. "

Shane continued to work until the horse would accept the rope around his middle with no fuss. Shane stopped at this point to explain all he had just been doing allowing the horse to sniff his hand and gave him a rub on his nose. Shane then produced a bareback pad, Running Wind reacted even worse to this than the ropes and was again running round Shane as he flicked the pad all over him, nevertheless Shane continued. Suddenly Running Wind stopped; Shane immediately rubbed the horse on his nose and left the bareback pad just resting gently on his back.

"Look!... now he is licking and chewing with his mouth. This is a good sign that he is learning and has taken on board what I want him to do."For a while the pair just stood. Cowboy and horse together.

Then as Shane again moved the pad Running Wind moved forward and looked set to start dancing around again...he hesitated though, and as he did so Shane again rubbed him and left the pad lying still on the horse's back. Soon Shane could move the pad all round the horse and he would remain standing still. Shane then worked on flexing the horses head round to the left and the right using the rope. Working also on backing the horse up and circling him –walking him forward by tapping him gently on the back with the non flexible stick. To the amusement of the crowd Shane actually rubbed his own body on the horse on his legs with his own legs and on his withers and back with his own shoulders and arms. All this work to prepare the horse was truly rewarded as after only a bare hour Shane jumped up and leant over the horse on each side. Running Wind was a little tense but none the less stood very still. The crowd was silent with their own tension and expectation as gently Shane sat upright on the horse. Keeping the single rope over to one side Shane encouraged the horse to bend in a tight circle on each side. Then sitting comfortably and easily on the horse with only a bareback pad and using a string halter and one long rope Shane rode calmly around the arena on each rein. Progressing now to a trot Shane even had to tap Running Wind on the hind quarter to get him to advance. Everyone watched awed as horse and rider trotted and cantered round. Then, as a superb finale Shane moved back on the horse then slowly as if asking permission he stood upright on the rear quarters of the horse his arms out and raised his hat to the crowd. Such a demonstration was truly impressive less than two hours after this "wild horse" was led into the arena.

Natalie was unbelievably impressed and moved by the colt start demonstration. When Shane at the end had stood up on Running Winds back the audience had given him a standing ovation.

High up on the stands an old man blew his nose and prepared to leave. As he passed the arena a loud squeal met his ears and Shane nearly lost control of Running Wind for the first time that evening. Bill stopped dead, unable to breathe --the horse was whickering to him! Shane turned and addressed the man.
"This horse knows you!"
Bill was hesitant but finally admitted, "Oh yes! I was present at his birth and I looked after him for five years."
"Come over here....please," Shane requested.
Reluctant to draw attention to himself Bill moved a little closer. Whickering like a foal Running Wind was pawing the ground.
Shane passed the long rope to Bill.
Running Wind immediately moved forward and laid his nose on Bills chest.

Natalie appeared and watched from the background as Bill caressed Running Wind on his nose. The old man seemed so familiar and suddenly it came to Natalie that he had been with the horse at the race.

Poor Bill was nearly overcome since the fateful race life had not been kind to the old stockman –Peter had unceremoniously sacked him and at 66 another job had been elusive. Although he had been canny with his money he had never owned a house and rental cottages were not cheap. He had been living with some other lads at a hostel nearby but knew he had to find a permanent home soon or end up on the streets. He had money invested in shares but had a secret reason for not wishing to touch it.

At this point Natalie approached…. Shane was charmed to witness this touching scene. With her quick understanding and sharp intelligence Natalie summed up the situation. If she could with diplomacy, pull it off, Natalie could solve several problems with one action… how best to broach the subject, though?

Shane however, had no such worries.

"Hey! Natalie, how would you like a groom for your horse!" Shane had seen immediately that Natalie would take a long while to be fully in control of Running Wind and on her own admission she was now becoming more and more involved in giving dance lessons. Her fame had spread and she could earn very good money. Running Wind still needed to be exercised every day and Shane could sense that given such a chance Bill would stick to the Quantum Savvy methods.

"Oh, yes, indeed I do, but where would I find someone who would work along with your methods Shane? I would never let Running Wind be looked after by just anyone."

"Aw… but Natalie we have the groom who brought your horse into the world See how Running Wind loves this guy."

Quickly taking the opening Shane had given her Natalie came in fast. "You were there when he was born?"

"Yes," Bill admitted, "The best foal I ever saw."

"Would you" she asked with great humility "be prepared to come and help look after him?"

Bill felt a tumult of emotions rise inside him; *this was just what he needed. Could he really be back with his boy again? It was as if the silken thread still held them tightly woven together.*

"I will ask Sue tomorrow --but as she has just lost a groom there could be work for her too and maybe a cottage." Natalie smiled at the old man.

Running Wind then took matters into his own hands as he nudged Bill towards Natalie; everyone laughed and said it was an omen.

Rob who had been talking to some other jockeys who had all been very impressed with the demonstration came over to find that Bill had secured a job and a delighted Natalie was overjoyed and praising Shane to anyone and everyone who would listen.

A horse is the projection of people's dreams about themselves-strong powerful and beautiful –and it has the capability of giving us escape from our mundane existence.
Pam Brown

Chapter 8

Natalie had joined the Quantum Savvy group and along with her inexpensive membership came coaching. When she received the first lesson and equipment pack through the post Natalie had been as thrilled as a child, at Christmas. To Sue's amusement the paper was no sooner off the new string halter and rope and long non flexible stick than Natalie was out in the arena trying it all out on Roxy. The Quantum Savvy study programme, Level 1 started with ground work, with a couple of ridden parts. To achieve her level 1 Natalie was required to practice and then film several different exercises with a horse – for this Natalie with Ellie's permission used Roxy.

Meredith Ransley was to be Natalie's coach and was very encouraging and definite about how Natalie should tackle the course. Sue and Ellie gave great support to Natalie although they did not really understand the methods used themselves. For Natalie the organised lessons complete with homework packs were a real bonus. Used to learning roles and being trained in general she took to the course easily.

The first assignment seemed too easy when she read the description.....*Approach your horses shoulder from 4 meters. Standing at or behind the shoulder allowing your horse to sniff the back of your hand. Rub your horse and ask them to bend towards you as you put your halter on and tie knot correctly, rub and check your horse all over. Pick up and check all 4 feet, time allowed 5 minutes.* Natalie had watched the DVD which came with the pack several times and seen how Shane and some of his students achieved this task. Catching Roxy was never difficult as she loved attention, but Natalie found it much harder than she had originally thought to get the horse to flex and bend her neck towards her... Rubbing Roxy was also easy as Natalie often gave her massages and she obviously enjoyed this. Roxy could, however, sometimes be difficult about giving her back feet. Natalie found she had to work harder than she had anticipated and in her first few attempts had taken a lot longer than the 5 minutes allowed.

Meredith was a very good coach and at first Natalie needed a lot of feedback the voice over video feedback was invaluable. As the level 1 assignments mounted up Meredith (with great insight into body language and horse behaviour) got the best from Natalie. Giving her encouragement and useful advice along the way. Ellie was a great help filming each assignment too... sometimes several times, which they then sent by internet to the Quantum Savvy web site. As the course progressed Natalie rarely needed to film the assignment more than once or twice.

Every time Natalie passed an assignment and earned a blue tick on her card she was thrilled, but she kept all this emotion inside. When she passed the final imagination challenge she was overjoyed. Finishing with a superb finale by loading then backing Roxy out of the horse box whilst sitting in a seat followed, circling Roxy round herself, then making the horse come sideways to the seat. Natalie then stood up on the chair and mounted Roxy bareback. She next demonstrated some sideways mounted moves, she backed the mare up, and finally slid grace-fully to the ground.

The 6 foot red string (to attach to her stick and replace her white one) was sent by Meredith as an honour of her passing Level 1. It was so precious to Natalie, as since her illness it was the first real accolade she had earned. With great energy and determination to continue as she had started, Natalie launched herself into the Level 2 part of the Quantum Savvy course; it was more intense involving work with the horse on a long 22ft line and bareback riding. Natalie was keen to progress but a lit-tle alarmed at some of the assignments she was going to have to master such things as cantering bareback on each rein for one minute and working with the horse at the end of a 22 ft line. De-termined not to be put off Natalie Launched herself into this work with renewed energy.

Natalie led Roxy into the arena and spent a few minutes ca-ressing her horse and swinging the savvy string all over her and round her legs. She then practiced a few flexes to the right and left and then backed up Roxy gently a couple of times. Her new 22ft long rope was startlingly white next to the shorter one which she had been using these last few months. The home-work card had said *back your horse to the end of the rope, bring him back in then back your horse over a pole.* Used to backing Roxy to the end of the 12ft rope Natalie imagined this part was gong to be easy. Roxy backed up about halfway before she stopped, making Natalie shake the rope harder. Eventually after several tries she had Roxy at the end of the rope. When she first she asked the horse to return to her Roxy planted her feet and raised her nose in defiance. Frustrated Natalie started shaking the rope and waving her stick and string. This simply caused

Roxy to brace even more and raise her head higher. Realising that she was getting nowhere Natalie sat down to think. *What had Meredith said--- at the end of this rope you will be testing your horses respect for you and if your aids are too heavy your horse will become dull.*

That was what Roxy was telling her; her aids were heavy and she was not being consistent enough a leader. Thus her horse lacked respect for her. Natalie decided to go backwards with this and asked Roxy very politely and gently with a small wiggle of the rope to go backwards just a few steps. Every time Roxy backed up a couple of steps Natalie immediately relaxed the tension on the rope as an instant reward for the horses try. After a half an hour she had worked up to sending Roxy about 18ft from her. Instead of going on to get to the end of the rope Natalie decided to leave it there. She easily brought Roxy in and rewarded her with lots of caresses and a lovely massage.

Within two weeks Natalie could back Roxy to the end of the rope, send her off in a circle in either direction, change direction and circle her over a jump with ease.

The next set of skills Natalie studied was to start liberty work. For this she needed a small round pen. Bill and Tom obligingly set up a portable round pen in a flat corner of one of the hay fields made possible now that the hay had been cut, baled and brought in. Natalie could use this space for several weeks.

Once you can do all your basic skills with the belly of your rope on the ground you can try them at liberty –keep it simple at first by just doing the three basic skills –If you have any trouble, go back on line for a while .

Natalie was not ready for the truths she found when she first removed the rope and halter. Roxy stood quiet and still while Natalie caressed her in a no yield with her hands and the stick and string. As soon as she asked for a hindquarter yield to her hands Roxy started to move round. Then as if realising for the first time that she was free of the rope she simply walked away from Natalie and stood at the gate to the round pen. As directed in the Lesson 5 hand book she simply put Roxy back on line and repeated all of her yields. Then when Natalie tried again without the line she got a very nice hindquarter yield from Roxy on each side. Deciding to stop then and let Roxy absorb all they had done Natalie led the big horse to her field.

Bill, whom Natalie was now relying upon to look after Running Wind was just coming out with her horse so she stayed to watch. Shane need not have worried, Bill was so grateful at being given this chance he literally ate up all the knowledge and information on the Quantum Savvy methods of horsemanship. Natalie bought Bill a TV and DVD player for which Shane and Meredith sent training discs. Despite his age Bill lapped it all up and was amazed at the results –guilty as most horse people are of having used brutal methods to achieve his ends in the past Bill was a true convert enthusing eloquently about Quantum Savvy on Friday nights to his mates in the local pub.

Bill had progressed even further with his charge than Natalie; he had run through quickly the Level 1 ground tasks with Running Wind and was especially proud of being able to ask his horse to load by just pointing at the trailer. When Bill removed the halter and rope his boy stayed willingly with his trainer. Natalie saw how good and passive a leader Bill was and how Running Wind chose to stay with him. The horse so obviously had great respect for the man. When Bill removed his halter and rope Running Wind did not move at all. Realising Natalie was watching Bill decided to run through some of the tasks for the assignment he knew Natalie was working on. It seemed the man only had to look at Running Winds hind quarter for the horse to do a beautiful yield the same with the fore quarter. As

115

Bill moved forwards; so too did the horse when Bill stopped so did Running Wind. Moving to the centre of the round pen, Bill asked his horse by raising his hand and pointing to his right to circle round him. The horseman's stick redundant by his side he did not need it. The first time he asked his horse in by yielding his hind and driving his horse in. Running Wind did not hesitate and confidently returned. Sent off easily in the other direction this time Bill asked the horse to come in by yielding his fore quarters and be drawn in. Natalie realised she had a lot of effort and work to put in to be even half as good as Bill. The calm polite way he asked Running Wind for something impressed Natalie and she resolved to be more like that with Roxy next time.

Natalie stood enchanted. Since she had bought the broken down Running Wind she had become more and more interested in horses, but she had never seen anything like this. Tom turned to her whispering.

"Thought you'd like it. This is a Prix St Georges competition so a very high level. But dressage can be performed at many different levels."

"Tom, it is superb. The horse...well, he's dancing like I used to only somehow it is better. The music changed tempo and the rider took his horse into a beautiful piaffe."

Natalie was spellbound. This was it.... this was what she wanted to do. She saw it now; rescuing Running Wind, watching him heal, learning to ride, working on the Quantum Savvy horsemanship course with Shane and Meredith It all made sense now.....dressage that was her direction now .

As Bill worked with Running Wind every day leading him out working him on the ground, literally playing games with him. Natalie continued with her riding lessons. Sue started to push Natalie now and one day suggested that Natalie tried a small dressage competition which was to be held locally. Although she was not sure if she was ready Natalie agreed. With her professional life becoming settled, Natalie realised that her personal life was not so sure. Both Jeremy and Rob had featured strongly in her recovery and she realised that both were actually, if she admitted to it, very important to her. Thinking that anything even remotely connected to romance could wait, Natalie decided to take Sue's recommendation and put all her energies into the dressage competition.

Natalie's life was revolving around her dance lesson pupils and horses. She now watched Bill working Running Wind at least twice a week. She and Bill had a real father daughter relationship. Bill worshiped Running Wind, knowing he would be the last horse he would work with and he was daily impressed with how the Quantum Savvy methods were transforming this horse. Natalie loved Running Wind with immense passion, but she knew she was still far from controlling him as Bill could.

Ellie was waiting for Natalie when she next came to the yard.

"Mum says you are going to enter for the Mid Counties dressage competition."

"Yes I don't know if I am ready yet."

"Will you let me help you and be your groom?" Ellie enthused.

Touched Natalie immediately agreed.

"Right," said Ellie "Mum says you need to concentrate on your transitions. I know all about those and Roxy can be lazy Lets see if I can help you."

"I know it's only a small competition," Natalie replied. "But I do want to do well. It would be a lovely way of thanking your mother."

Despite being only a small local competition there were quite a few entries and as soon as it was known that Natalie was competing spectator numbers were set to be high. Bill encouraged all his racing mates to support Natalie, Jeremy's entire family were due to watch and all Natalie's dance pupils were coming too.

This may have been intimidating had Natalie not spent 5 years as a top ballerina -- used to the limelight and being watched actually helped Natalie and spurred her on.

A rare blue sky with bright sunshine greeted the spectators for the Novice dressage competition, Little Coombe Halt village was a lovely setting, and surprisingly a very large crowd was gathering. All horse events have their usual aficionados and this event was no different. Several riders had performed at this event before and were expectant of similar results again. Some had been intrigued to see an entry from a rider unknown to their clique.... no chance they all said laughing.

The horse boxes were rolling in and riders beginning to back their horses out of the trailers. Some were lunging them actively, in aggressive circles, with the poor creatures unaware of what was actually required of them. Into this clique of uppity riders Natalie arrived. Her first ever show! As such she was completely unaware of how competitors normally behave. Flanked by Sue, Ellie, and Rob, Natalie was not even looking at what the other riders were doing. She had emailed Meredith a few days before the event to ask advice on the best preparation and exactly what she should do with Roxy using Quantum Savvy methods therefore she was completely focused on what she was doing. Roxy was quietly unloaded and allowed to relax and graze the somewhat lush grass around- noticing that the other competitors seemed hell bent on preventing their horses from eating. When Roxy was calm Natalie started playing with her. At first she just caressed the big gentle horse all over – Roxy was nervous because of the journey and all the noise around her. Natalie sensed that she would have to work for a while until Roxy was as relaxed and receptive as usual. As she was de - sensitising Roxy by hand, string and stick several of the usual and local riders passed by to watch. Natalie was not even aware of them but they only watched for a short while before moving on in two's or threes, bitching vociferously about the new comer and her weird methods.

Perhaps the best thing for Natalie was her complete naivety. She had never been to a dressage competition before, so she had no preconceived ideas. Although Sue felt a little embarrassed by Natalie's attitude, Ellie and Rob made up for this by their complete support. Natalie's wait to enter the ring was three quarters of an hour, so instead of watching the others while her horse was waiting tied to the horse box as most competitors did, she worked Roxy by Quantum Savvy methods desensitising, yielding by contact and non contact, flexing, backing, achieving great relaxation and lightness in her horse. She soon had Roxy listening and circling round with good impulsion.

When finally Natalie's name was called she calmly walked Roxy to the collecting ring, the rider before her was just waiting to go in --- to Natalie's amazement it took two people to help this woman control her horse. It was so tense that it was circling and fidgeting. As the stressed horse jog trotted into the arena, Natalie caressed Roxy all over again until she really was calm. Rob was still holding her horse by the reins. When Natalie said "let her go." The stewards watched amazed as Natalie threw Roxy's reins on her withers – she then mounted her horse with no aid standing quietly as if asking permission with one foot in the stirrup before swinging her leg over. Roxy stood rock still not moving an inch. As a result of her calm approach to warm up Roxy worked in beautifully in the intervening 10 minutes before she was due to present herself for the test.

The tannoy announced Natalie's name riding Roxy and she walked slowly and calmly to the arena. Years of learning and memorising ballets meant that Natalie was not about to make a silly mistake about the programme. As the music started Natalie felt as if the horse was almost asking her *what do you want?* Sue watched with her daughter standing hand in hand, Rob hovering behind. Roxy excelled, always a horse with fluid and light movements. It appeared as if Roxy knew what today was all about and truly wanted Natalie to win – her extended trot was a marvel to watch and her halt and back up faultless. The horse was so light and responsive. Natalie was unaware of the stir she had caused as she left the arena and gave Roxy her head. As the tannoy reverberated with the point's results Natalie was unsaddling her horse herself and gently caressing her. Fury was abroad and faces red with indignation were bitching – the fact remained though that Natalie had won a clear victory and the one thing not one of the dissenters could refute was the impeccable behaviour of Roxy compared to their own horses.

Sensing the atmosphere Sue decided that a quick exit would avoid any nastiness but she was not quite quick enough. A red faced, slightly overweight woman was approaching. Sue knew Rose Elliott. President of the local Riding club and set to win here normally as she had done for the last four years. This year not only had Natalie pipped her to the top place but Rose's horse had bucked during her turn – *not quite Quantum Savvy* Sue reflected wryly – she was becoming more and more converted to Quantum Savvy ways every day and Natalie's win had pushed her over the literal edge. Rose launched in verbally at Natalie about weird methods and interfering newcomers and how Roxy must be drugged to behave as she did. Sue expected the quiet gentle Natalie to be put down and intimidated by this tirade. Instead everyone witnessed a fury unleashed as Natalie spun round on Rose "Drugged is she? Oh no she is not – nor is she beaten, abashed, and misunderstood as your horse is. Ok if she is drugged to be calm, you go ahead and ride her. Rose backed away from this and looked almost afraid –"Go on!" Natalie insisted. "You just said it. She is drugged so just get on. She won't move." Sue nervously watched this. She knew that although quiet and calm with someone she knew and trusted, Roxy could be explosive if stressed. Quite a crowd had gathered. Along with Rose's cronies, Jeremy and his family, Bill and quite a few of his stable mates were there; jeering started and Rose knew she would have to get on this horse or admit defeat. Backing down now would leave Natalie victor in more ways that one. Entirely confident that Roxy must have been drugged to remain so calm and let Natalie mount her so easily, Rose took up the challenge…. Sue was unhappy but Ellie, as owner, led the mare up and winked conspiratorially at her mother. Sue remembered Roxy hates loud voices. One of the reasons Natalie and Roxy were so good together was how quiet Natalie always was around her, one shout and Roxy could be unpredictable. Rose took Roxy's reins with a crowd gathering by the minute *"Stand back all of you"* she shouted and Roxy flinched. Rose then took Roxy's reins tight and asked one of her cronies to help her mount. As her seat hit the saddle hard Roxy set off towards the arena entrance bucking and circling then bolting forwards – one final buck ditched Rose unceremoniously on the ground. As she stood brushing the dust from her clothes – a snigger of laughter was inevitably starting. Suddenly Natalie appeared in the arena. Ignoring Rose completely she moved slowly towards Roxy…silence fell as the crowd watched. Natalie gently took Roxy's reins and caressed her. It was as if there was no one else there as she worked Roxy by hand as she did not have the stick and string. After 10 minutes Roxy started mirroring Natalie's lateral move-ments. When Natalie felt her mare was ready she jumped up and down next to Roxy on each side then calmly mounted her. Roxy stood rock still again and Natalie then rode Roxy calmly round the arena at a walk, trot and canter. The crowd was cheering again and for the second time Natalie realised that she had won.

Jeremy and Annabel approached Natalie as she was leaving the arena. For once Annabel's scathing comments were welcome, in an intended to be overheard voice as she berated the bitches. "There's a distinct smell of Rose...hanging in the air," and "I didn't know they held Rodeo classes here! "

"Fantastic! Natalie. You truly showed them." Jeremy enthused. "Now you must come out for a meal with us all this evening."

Rob who had been standing close shrank backwards into the crowd at this. His joy at watching Natalie's double victory clouded by watching Natalie and Jeremy together; her eyes seemed to light up when Jeremy was near.

The wind of heaven is that which blows between a horse's ears.
Arab proverb

Chapter 9

Rob was still paying a weekly visit ostensibly to see Running
Wind and this would be his first chance to tell Natalie how
proud he was of her wins at the dressage competition. As he
approached Sue's Yard he saw that the whole family were
ranged around the outdoor school. Curious, Rob approached to
see Bill in the school working Running Wind who was wearing
Natalie's dressage saddle. It was obvious how much work Bill
had put in, as he worked him at liberty the horse mirrored his
every move and changed direction or backed up at a small signal from Bill.

Natalie stood watching, her eyes never leaving Running
Wind….she was dressed in Jodhpurs and holding a hat.

Rob sensed that he was about to witness a special event.

"Oh, Rob, you are here!" Natalie cried when she saw him.
"We were just waiting for you."

Sue turned to Rob. "Bill is working Running Wind for a while
then Natalie will work him and this will be her first ride on him.
She has passed her Level 2 with Roxy so now she wants to concentrate on her Level 1 with Running Wind; she has to do the
two ridden assignments."

Rob was unaware that Natalie had even been working her
horse on the ground so was taken aback to say the least. Never-

theless Natalie's admission that they had been waiting for him was heart warming.

Bill signalled to Natalie and she entered the arena. Bill had the string halter and long 12ft line in his hand. He gently put the halter on Running Wind and handed the line to Natalie. Standing up straight Natalie started to work desensitising the horse by swinging the long rope then the stick and string all around the horse over his neck and back round his legs. Yielding his forequarters and hind quarters. She then worked on flexing him and backing him up. Running Wind seemed calm and trusting with Natalie. Bill returned to the arena and stood by the horse but he did not touch him....he just stood close. Natalie then jumped up and down next to the horse on both sides and then slowly mounted. She sat gently in the saddle and, using the single rope set off on a direct rein around the arena just walking. Rob felt that the sound of a pin dropping would have been loud as not one word was said; everyone was so aware and connected to the scene. Rob himself was very moved he knew Natalie had waited a long time for this. He alone had always known she wanted to ride her horse and together they were indeed beautiful. The horse's sleek coat gleamed in the late afternoon sun showing the reddish tints on the light bay background and Natalie was a picture of poise and elegance sitting demurely astride him. Rob reflected upon Running Winds life and wondered what the people in the yards he had passed through would think if they could witness this cameo. *The horse they believed to be dangerous and unbalanced being ridden by a tiny ballerina with no bit and only one long rope.*

Ellie was snapping photos like mad with her digital camera while her parents just stood by watching.

For the first time as he watched Natalie ride gracefully round on Running Wind Rob admitted to himself how important she had become in his life. When he realised that just for once Jeremy was not there and that Natalie had been waiting for him he allowed himself some small measure of hope but he knew how influential and rich Jeremy was, the thought intimidated him.

"What?" the small lad flinched as Peter Lake shouted at him.

"Running Wind- you know that difficult horse we had here what fell in the Gold cup was in the yard I last worked for!" he repeated.

Staring into the fire Peter Lake poured himself another whisky, finishing the bottle.

His horse—Running Wind was his horse -he should be here in his yard, winning money for him –badly needed money. That was it. How to save his yard! Get that horse racing for him again! After all, that stupid interfering girl didn't deserve him –easy job though for Peter to get him back.

As he opened another bottle Peter picked up the phone – he knew people –people he really shouldn't know.

Rob couldn't believe it. God what could he possibly say to Natalie. He had to call her straight away. Although it was only 6.00 in the morning he had to tell her Running Wind was gone – missing-- his stable empty.

Chaos met Natalie as she drove fast into the yard.

Ellie ran to meet her and she saw Rob with Sue also moving towards her

Sue was in great distress and Rob also looked very upset.

"We have no idea where he could have gone," Rob admitted.

Natalie ran to Running Wind's stable and sank to her knees in the straw. The smell of horse was still strong, but the large stable was cold and empty. Later Bill who was as distressed as

125

Natalie was to promise to her that he would find Running Wind.

The George and Dragon at 900pm on a Friday evening was full of lads aspiring to be jockeys. Most of whom would not only never be jockeys, but who would not even last the life of being lads.

Bill had kept apace of who worked where. He had his own suspicions about the missing horse. It was no secret among the lads that Peter Lake had hit the bottle seriously and could not keep either lads or horses in training for long.

When Joey walked in Bill called him over to the bar, giving the impression of being well inebriated, Bill offered the weak young lad a drink. Having spent all his money on betting, Joey readily accepted a drink. Bill was canny and suffered Joeys childish ranting about his life while buying him two more drinks – offering a 'chaser' whiskey with the third pint was to produce the required result for Bill when Joey started spilling the beans about the new horse in the yard. Bill had to ball his fists in his pockets and hold his tongue as the young lad described how they had to control the new powerful uncooperative horse – "And the bugger will squeal when he doesn't like something," Joey whined.

Bill had heard enough, but fed yet another drink to the unsuspecting Joey and talked the routine of the yard out of him.

Rob and Jeremy, although polite in to each other in company, were not exactly best of friends. Nonetheless they had spent several hours together and were planning to pull off a great stunt together – king pin in their scheme was Natalie who was far from sure she could complete her part, but her love for Running Wind fired her with determination – she had saved him once. She would do so as many times as he needed her.

Early evening on a Sunday is a quiet time with the horses in their stables and usually any lads at the stables having a rest.

Peter Lake had been excited ever since the call this morning. This could be it! The break he needed. Lord Castle wanted to bring two of his horses here to train.

As Jeremy's chauffeur drove the Rolls into the yard, Bill and Rob were busy manoeuvring the Land Rover and horse box belonging to Sue into the small nearby hamlet as close as they could to Peter's yard .

Dressed to kill Natalie stepped from the Rolls helped out by Jeremy. She was wearing tight stretch trousers, a tight jumper and smart jacket a bit like a hacking jacket, complete with a floppy hat and dark sun glasses. She looked every inch the rich Lord Castle's girlfriend! She was also carrying a small shoulder bag and wearing ballet type pumps. Natalie sincerely hoped Peter Lake would not remember her from Cheltenham all those months ago. She need not have feared not only had she gained weight and grown her hair longer but the already inebriated trainer was not paying much attention to her at all.

Playing the part of the woman who knows nothing about horses -Natalie asked if she could visit the stables –"Good idea darling." Jeremy encouraged.

Peter did not really wish anyone to see Running Wind, but could not easily prevaricate and he was sure he was safe as not many people would know the horse but he steered Jeremy swiftly away.

In truth apart from Running Wind there were only two has been race horses, one hack and his neighbour's daughters jump- ing pony in the yard.

Natalie stopped at the pony's stable and then produced a car- rot from her pocket. The pony extended its lips and sucked the carrot up crunching it loudly.

Jeremy turned back to Natalie and in a dismissive and chauvinistic voice said "Yes, darling...you just feed some carrots to the horses, Peter and I have some business to do."

"Oh, yes, I love giving them carrots," Natalie obediently replied.

Mentally rubbing his hands on a deal Peter was delighted to see Jeremy was a man after his own heart and considered that women did not know anything about horses.

Natalie watched them go inside. She took in the layout of the yard. A lad was just finishing his chores and she dutifully fed a carrot to each horse including Running Wind, who whickered softly to her. The lad washed up a couple of buckets, closed up the top doors and then went off towards the house. Sitting on a wall, Natalie saw him reappear 10 minutes later and head off down the road towards the pub. Bill had offered to pay for a couple of drinks for Joey to be sure he would be out of the yard.

Knowing she did not have long Natalie worked fast. From her bag she took a thin string halter and an equally slim 6 foot rope which was all she had managed to fit in. She hid the bag in a bucket and quietly entered Running Wind's stable. Remembering wryly when just putting a halter on the horse was difficult she worked quickly and gently put the halter on with a soft flex, she gave another carrot to Running Wind.

Praying that Jeremy was speaking as loudly as he had promised to and generously pouring the 18 yr old whisky he had brought, she led the horse out of the stable which she then closed up as if the horse were still there; bouncing up and down next to the horse she then vaulted onto his back.

Bill had said he thought it would take her about a half hour to reach the lane where Rob waited with the horse box.

Natalie had only ridden Running Wind a few times before and had never ridden him bareback – she had however spent quite some hours on Roxy with no saddle. As they left the yard it was as if her horse sensed the need for silence which was acute in Natalie. Out of the yard up the lane and then cross the river... was the route Bill had given her. It seemed to be going well as they walked out quickly, but when they got to the end of the lane a large dog stepped out in front of them barking and running forwards at them he was dragging a long and heavy chain which made a horrible grating noise. Running Wind shied and veered sideways nearly unseating Natalie, then instead of crossing the river he set off along the river bank. Natalie had only the one long rope but she did not panic, she sat back and thought of stopping. Running Wind slowed, Natalie did not really want to stop, so she thought about being at the other side of the river. Although the crossing was deeper and more difficult further up stream Running Wind entered the water willingly and they were soon in the copse on the other side. Worried now that they would miss the rendezvous site Natalie started trotting the horse....

When Rob heard the hoof beats further up the lane than he had thought he turned and looked. Amazed he saw Natalie bareback trotting Running Wind calmly along the lane. Relieved to see him she jumped down and handed over the horse to Rob.

Not even greeting him properly she set off on foot back in the direction she had come from. Natalie's one worry about the return had been crossing the river. However, because she had come higher up stream she had seen a bridge a small foot bridge a little further on. Running fast now and, more importantly, staying dry she crossed the river and made her way back up the lane. As luck would have it the dog was gone and Natalie returned to the yard unseen.

Recovering both her bag and her breath, Natalie brushed the dust off her clothes and sat posed on the wall reading a fashion magazine – Jeremy's idea borrowed from Annabel.

A bare three minutes later Jeremy and Peter returned to the Yard. It was quite clear to Natalie that Peter was very worse the wear from drink and even Jeremy gave the impression of having indulged.

In response to a mobile phone signal Jones, Jeremy's chauffeur returned and Natalie quickly climbed back into the car. Jeremy shook hands with Peter once more and he, too, got back into the car. As the Rolls cruised out of the yard Natalie sank sideways into Jeremy's arms, a huge grin on her face.

Watching them go Peter Lake smirked to himself it had been easy. *Lord Castle was coming back on Wednesday with the first horse. Just in time as the bailiffs letter had only given him until the end of the week.* At 6.30 on a Sunday night Peter would normally have gone round the boxes and checked the horses for the night, but Jeremy had deliberately left the bottle on the table. Shrugging he turned back into the house; *after all what could possibly be wrong with any of the horses?*

Sue replaced the kettle and cut generous slices of cake for everyone as they sat around the table to hear Natalie's tale.

"He was superb as if he knew what was happening until we met the dog but that only spooked him a little bit. He remained focused on me and as I was bareback I could feel him listening to my every move."

"He was so calm when he went into the horse box," Bill enthused "I think he really wanted to come home."

"Oh, Bill, don't be modest! He whickered like a foal when he saw you nearly pulled me over to get to you!" Rob teased.

They all laughed! Running Wind's love for Bill was a yard joke. They said he wouldn't even eat without Bill, "Ah, but

Natalie is becoming increasingly important to him lately," Bill sadly confessed.

"Yes, they looked like one as they came up the lane." Rob added looking away as Natalie turned to him shyly with her eyes lowered.

Love won't be tampered with, love won't go away. Push it to one side and it creeps to the other.
Louise Erdrich

Chapter 10

The last two years had been the best in Natalie's life, while she was dancing it was her whole world taking up nearly every waking moment in one form or another. Her home life with Stefan, she reflected, had been shallow and his verbal abuse and childish domineering behaviour left little room for enjoyment. Now she had a much more fulfilling life. Teaching dance gave her the connection with ballet without the demanding commitments. Her growing love for her horse and riding him gave her an inner peace and joy she had never experience before. The co-ordinated rescue of Running Wind where she, Rob and Jeremy, Bill and Sue had all participated together showed her the good close friends they had all become. She felt safe and comfortable in her cottage and spent the time she was not teaching or riding in her garden. Sue sometimes teased her that she needed a man in her life, but- could she ever imagine sharing her life with anyone again after Stefan. Her bruised emotions must have healed by now; she tried hard to envisage living her life with a man again. *If I ever do-- it will be for love and because I cannot live my life without him.*

Sometimes fate helpfully precipitates matters; just this week she had received two very different invitations which had her mind in turmoil. From Jeremy's mother, a very formal invitation, in beautiful script on a cream coloured card to a dinner party at Woodstock House that Friday. She was invited to stay for the night as the party would start late. Dress formal the card had read- sending Natalie into a nervous confusion. The second invitation conversely was from Rob who offered a casual telephone invitation for her to eat with him. "If you are brave enough" he had laughed "I will cook for you." Coincidentally the invitation was for the Saturday evening following the dinner party and Rob had added that there would be just the two of them.

This had sent Natalie into a very reflective mood, both Jeremy and Rob were very important to her, she had the impression they each in their own way wanted to look after her, but also were looking for more. If she was truthful to herself she saw Jeremy in a more avuncular light; friend of the family for so long, protector, gentle advisor. That he was undoubtedly more handsome and a great deal richer than Rob was true. Still Natalie was not convinced she wanted closeness with either of them. *Why can't it just stay as it is* she thought to herself. In reality Jeremy was now 38 and had confessed to Natalie one day that his mother was making noises about an heir to the title and Estate. He had looked strangely at Natalie as he said this and she realised he was on the brink of proposing to her. Reacting as she always did when embarrassed and compromised she quickly made her excuses and rather rudely rushed off. For a while Jeremy had been a little stiff and cold towards her, making her regret her behaviour, but she just could not imagine turning him down, better if he never asked her at all.

Sue had been a great help, since Natalie had told her of the invitations. Firstly she had laid her own kitchen table with a stunning array of knifes and forks. After explaining about each one and when to use it she drilled Natalie on imaginary dishes until Natalie knew exactly what to use when. She also gave Natalie a crash course in social manners and conversation. Jeremy had filled her in about the guests. Lady Castle had sent a guest list round, carefully indicating who was invited; to which she had mysteriously added at the bottom `surprise guest `.

"Major Rivers has a great fondness for the bottle, don't what ever you do let him mix you a cocktail, his wife is a wee mouse of a thing but there isn't a horse in the county she can't ride, you will be able to talk with her for hours about Running Wind. She was very excited when she heard you were coming. Sir Gerald Caruthers is I'm afraid a bit of a bore but he will spend most of the evening filling up his considerable bulk with food and drink, his wife is very old fashioned so do mind your ps and qs talking to her. The vicar is very pleasant and his wife is sweet--- if we keep her off the sherry." At this point Natalie started to laugh. Jeremy joined in with a chuckle then went on. Then there are the Bourn-Rogers. He's all right a fellow lawyer, but she is a bit giggly and nervous and apt sometimes to put her pretty little foot right in it. Clare and Annabel will be there mother of course. Oh- and my uncle Stanley and my cousin Giles, Stanley's son. His wife my Aunt Matilda and their daughter cousin Bryony are in London so will not be here.

Realising that this was to be a very formal dinner Natalie was even more grateful to Sue. Last night she had confessed to Sue and Ellie about Rob's invitation.

"One on Friday one on Saturday" she mused "Not even a few days apart, never mind weeks."

"You should thank your lucky stars my girl" Sue remonstrated. "Two handsome eligible bachelors both courting you in competition with each other."

Startled, Natalie said hesitatingly "Do you really think they see each other as rivals?"

"Of course they do, but don't worry. I think somehow there will be no duels at dawn."

"Well." Ellie put in "If it was down to Running Wind to choose, Jeremy wouldn't get a look in, apart from Bill and Natalie no one else but Rob ever gets even a whicker from that horse!"

Sue called up stairs where Ellie was helping Natalie put her hair up that Jeremy's Rolls had arrived. Natalie knew she should be happily looking forward to this evening. A ride in the country in the luxurious Rolls, which was filled with snacks, magazines and a full drinks cabinet. Then a sumptuous dinner with champagne and fine wines. She was more nervous than she had been for years, and who exactly was this mystery guest. It would seem that only Jeremy's mother knew the identity of this guest, Jeremy himself had no idea but did not seem too perturbed." Another attempt at a match for Annabel probably, she never learns and still keeps trying despite the string of disastrous results." This comment reassured Natalie a little, but meeting all these new people was intimidating and so her drive to Oxfordshire was uneasy.

Having only been in the kitchen and small parlour of Jeremy's house before, Natalie was not ready for the grandeur of the formal lounge. She was frankly stunned by the table seen through a high arch with gleaming silver candelabras in which Ivory coloured candles were burning. Her gratitude to Sue was immense as her gaze caught the puzzling array of cutlery on the table.

Jeremy took her arm and led her towards a couple near the fireplace; she recognised them from his description before he even introduced them to her.

"Major Bernard and Mrs Helen Rivers" Turning to Natalie he added "May I introduce Natalie Diaz." As they all shook hands politely exchanging platitudes Jeremy signalled his butler who was carrying a silver tray of champagne flutes. He handed round the glasses, by now all the guests had a glass and they drank a toast to their hostess; Jeremy's mother who was standing close.

As Natalie sipped her wine, the butler came back up to Jeremy and whispered something to him. Laying his glass down on a table he turned back to Natalie "It seems our mystery guest has arrived, please excuse me I must go and do my duty." Jeremy seemed bemused as he walked off.

Grabbing her arm Helen Rivers pulled Natalie closer to herself as the Major, having downed his glass of champagne in one gulp picked up Jeremy's abandoned one and strode off.

"My dear, I have been eagerly waiting to meet you now tell me all about this marvellous horse of yours" Sighing, Natalie started to tell the story, as she knew it of Running Wind. She did not get far, as soon as she mentioned his difficult early personality Helen Rivers cut in.

"Now I had a mare like that –Chestnut 16 .3 she was, out of our own Night Time lady- you know from the Irish jumping Kingdom lines. A devil she was in the begining, must say I never thought I get round Badminton on her the first time I took her, but she was a great jumper bold as brass."

Relieved, Natalie realised she would not have to do much talking and indeed 10 minutes later when Jeremy re appeared with a tall dark haired woman on his arm. Helen was going round another three day event on a different horse describing each fence as if it was yesterday. It must have been 40 years ago Natalie thought as the Rivers looked to be in their seventies.

Intrigued by Jeremy and this new arrival, Natalie let Helen's continuing descriptions of endless horses and bloodlines and events trickle past her consciousness. Trying to watch without seeming to, and still appear interested in Helens ramblings, was not easy. However she saw enough to see that the appearance of this very attractive woman had disturbed Jeremy in some way. They spoke in hushed whispers for quite some time then suddenly the woman broke away and headed for the downstairs cloakroom. Knowing that there were ample facilities for more than one woman, including three toilet booths and a large elegant make up area with gilt mirrors which had stunned her on her first visit, Natalie waited a discreet 5 minutes and also took her leave. A crestfallen Helen pleaded with her to please return, as she still had to tell her about her first stallion Normandy. Natalie made her way to the toilets and quietly entered. The woman, who seemed as if she had been crying, looked at Natalie when she came in then quickly looked away. Making her way to the mirror while digging in her bag for her lipstick Natalie tried to seem casual.

"Hello I'm Natalie Diaz." Politely she held out her hand. The woman took it reluctantly but did not look at her.

"Katherine Chandler."

"The water colour artist? "

"Yes! - But how have you heard of me? "

"I was a ballet dancer for many years with the Barbican Ballet; everyone wanted one of your paintings. No one has ever captured the grace and poise, pain and dedication each ballet dancer puts into their work as you can. I particularly like your studies in one colour wash of students at the exercise bar." At this the woman looked a little gratified but she still held her triste air.

137

"How do you come to know Jeremy then? "Katherine asked in a strained voice.

"He was my father's lawyer – normally a family such as ours couldn't afford a lawyer like Jeremy. But my father was working for a firm in London making chairs. This was his speciality and he was very good at it. The boss of the firm had a legal wrangle going on with a client and Jeremy was in charge of the case. He came to see my father's boss one day when the boss was out. My father was so engrossed in the detailed work on the chair he was making he didn't even notice Jeremy for ages. When finally he realised Jeremy was there he was embarrassed. Jeremy reassured him there was no harm done and complimented him richly on his work. A few weeks later Jeremy's secretary told him there was a *working man* as she put it outside with a parcel under his arm. Ushered into Jeremy's office my father stood before him with a brown paper wrapped parcel. Hesitantly he said. "I have a proposition for you." As he spoke he unwrapped the parcel revealing a magnificent chair. `I would like you to be our family lawyer if I can pay with chairs. You could call this an advanced payment. I have never made a will but maybe we could come to an arrangement.'Perhaps some Lawyers would have sent my father packing, but he had chosen well and Jeremy was delighted with the chair. I don't know how many chairs my father made for Jeremy over the years, but they became firm friends. Until I ended up in hospital I had only met Jeremy a few times, but now he has become a good friend. And you?" she asked in her turn. "How long have you known Jeremy?"

"Me ---- Oh I think I've been in love with Jeremy for most of my life, but recently he has had other distractions. I hardly ever see him." Kate had spoken so quietly that at first Natalie wasn't sure she hadn't misheard her. For the first time Kate looked directly at Natalie who was shocked by the raw agony she saw in her face. *So this is love, this is how it feels; I didn't ever even feel so strongly about Stefan.* Natalie was absolutely sure now that she was not and never had been in love with Jeremy. Indeed she loved and admired him as an uncle, certainly not with the intensity of feeling and passion that this woman did.

"And you think I am that distraction? "

"Aren't you? -- All I have heard is Natalie this, Running Wind and Natalie that –you and your precious horse that's all he talks about." As she said this Kate turned her head away, but not before Natalie saw that she was crying again.

Oh God what a mess! Natalie decided that she would put the record straight with Kate first, then try to speak with Jeremy later to see what his real feelings for Kate were.

"I am not in love with Jeremy, I never have been and I certainly do not wish to marry him –I have no intention of marrying anyone at the moment" –Fleeting images of Rob ran through her head, but she chased then away.

Kate looked up her expression hopeful, and then she looked sad and resigned again. "It wasn't Jeremy who invited me here tonight, it was Jeremy's mother. She has always wanted Jeremy to marry me. My father doesn't have a title but he is fabulously rich- so since Jeremy is already a Lord I would become Lady Castle, something my father would pay any amount to see."

"But Jeremy is also very rich. "

"I don't suppose you have any idea how much money it takes to keep an Estate like this. When Jeremy marries his mother wants to move to the dowager house. It has been empty for years inhabited by rats and bats. It will take a few hundred thousand to bring it up to Lady Castles standard. My father has made it quite clear that the renovation work costs would be covered entirely by him- should Jeremy and I marry. All was arranged so for years, until you came along."

"Well! As I have no intention of marrying Jeremy there's nothing stopping you."

"God! You are a stupid bitch! "Kate flung the words at Natalie "Can't you see it takes two to Tango – its you Jeremy loves not me."

She stormed out; leaving Natalie stunned realising how naive she had been.

It was actually a relief to be reclaimed by Helen Rivers when she returned to the lounge. It was also fortunate that the butler announced dinner just at that moment. Natalie happily walked in with the major who offered her his arm, even if he did seem a little unsteady on his feet. Natalie was placed between Helen Rivers on one side and John Bourne-Rogers on the other side. Facing her were Jeremy's cousin Giles and Debbie Bourne-Rogers.

Thanks to Sues coaching the dinner passed easily enough and Natalie allowed herself to relax a little. Finally the dessert was served, a spiced crème Brule with cinnamon cream and red fruit compote, with which the waiters served a rich Sauternes wine in elegant flutes. Almost as soon as she was served the wine, Debbie Bourne-Rogers gulped down half of her glass. Giggling she looked directly across the table at Natalie.

"Well" she slurred, leaning across the table. "When are you and Jeremy going to name the day" Leaning further forward but speaking in a louder voice she continued. "I musscht shay darling-- I do envy you- not only ish he the mossht dissshy man alive, but darling he's jusht loaded."

A stony reserved silence came over the table, chairs scraped and there were a few nervous coughs. Mortified Natalie was about to bolt from the table when Debbie Bourne-Rogers fell sideways off her chair. Giles was quick to react and easily lifted the skinny blonde woman and carried her out. "Tracy" Lady Castles voice rang out and one of the maids serving ran to her mistress side. "Mrs Bourne-Rogers has been taken poorly, please follow Giles and see she is settled in her bed."

With great dignity Lady Castle then called for the cheese platter and port. Natalie stole a glance discreetly from under her lashes, Lady Matlida Caruthers looked furious and ready to leave, Mr Bourne-Rogers was flushed and looked haughty, Katherine had turned pasty white, her eyes coal black as she watched Natalie: she looked tragic and resigned.

As the butler served the last course Natalie finally looked across at Jeremy. To her amazement he was staring at Katherine as if he had seen her for the first time this evening.

So much had happened in such a short time that Natalie was still trying to analyse it all on Saturday afternoon. Whenever she felt out of sorts Natalie took refuge in her relationship with her horse. Having arrived home just after noon and feeling too full to eat lunch she had driven straight to the stables. Bill greeted her with friendly enthusiasm. "He's in the home paddock I'll just get him for you, Sue wants to see you."

Natalie realised Sue would expect her to give a full account of the previous evenings proceedings. "Bill I haven't got much time lets just do a little ground work and maybe I will ride him bareback for a short ride."

The two spent twenty minutes working Running Wind on the ground as Natalie took him through his paces Bill was there encouraging and putting up new obstacles and setting new challenges. Finally Natalie mounted her horse from a plastic barrel she used for training. Only when she was trotting round on Running Wind, would she let herself try to analyse lasts nights dramatic scene.

After the undignified departure of Debbie Bourne-Rogers the remaining guests had been very reserved and most had retired quickly. The vicar and his wife were the only guests not staying, as the vicarage was so very close. Natalie escaped as soon as she could avoiding everyone's eyes especially Annabel's. Climbing the main staircase, following Tracy who was to show her to the bedroom prepared for her, she saw Jeremy and Kate standing close conversing in whispers. They stood in an alcove by the bay French windows partly lit by moonlight. Natalie could not tell in the dim light if their stance was romantic or not. Praying for their reunion she stole past.

In the morning Natalie was one of the first guests up and she took only black coffee which she drank in a strained silence with Annabel and Lady Castle.

At last Lady Castle broke the silence." I have arranged for my chauffeur to take you back to Newmarket in my Bentley Continental." She paused, looking directly at Natalie, "Jeremy needed his car to return early to London, he is due in court later this morning, Katherine Chandler has gone with him." The slightly condescending tone she used was accompanied by a gloating look in her eye, Natalie looked away to hide her amusement at the old lady's triumph. *If only you knew you supercilious old cow. I have no desire what so ever to marry your darling son. I will be as happy as you if Jeremy and Kate marry.*

Turning the shower up to its hottest setting Natalie let the steaming jet of water and fragrant shampoo wash last night's revelations away. Though she wanted to distance herself from the events, Natalie couldn't help re running the images in her head, she wanted a clear mind for this evening but the video would keep replaying. Could she? Would she? Ever feel as strongly about someone as Kate does for Jeremy.

If she was truthful to herself Natalie was looking forward to this evening. The idea of a more relaxed and intimate meal was less daunting. Robs first floor barn conversion was only a few miles away so Natalie called for a taxi knowing she was likely to drink more than just one glass of wine. Last night she had been so un nerved and self conscious she had taken only very small sips of wine and in the 5 hours the meal had lasted consumed less than two glasses.

Despite their long friendship Natalie had never been inside Rob's apartment, she knew where it was and had seen it from the outside on the occasions she had driven Rob home, often with racing injuries she thought wryly.

Framed in the doorway Rob seemed a little taller and even thinner if that was possible, his face lined and weather beaten. He wore tight slim black Jeans an open neck collarless shirt also black and a grey leather waistcoat. When he saw Natalie he grinned as she was wearing black trousers and a black top with a grey scarf.

"Snap!" He laughed as he ushered her in.

Natalie also laughed; glad this had removed any awkwardness. The flat was warm and inviting and smelt delicious. A table had been beautifully set in an alcove on which a red candle was flickering, over time dripping wax had nearly completely covered the glass forming crazy sculptures on the side. Rob conjured a bouquet of flowers as if by magic as Natalie handed him a bottle of Chateau Rothschild red wine.

Looking round Natalie could see that this was a true bachelor pad but it also had great charm. The comfortable looking deep red sofa and armchairs had exotic silk throws on them which were un doubtably from the far east. A beautiful dark Siamese cat was curled on a red silken cushion on one of the chairs in front of an open fireplace where fragrant logs were burning. On the cream coloured walls superb prints of horses and racing fought for place with paintings which she was sure were originals and a few photos. A large coloured photo stopped her short it showed a jockey obviously Rob standing high in the stirrups an ecstatic expression on his face one hand on the horse's mane in a caress and the other arm held high in a victory salute. Natalie studied the horse, dark with sweat; led by a grinning elderly man it had a lightning blaze.

Rob appeared behind her. "Yes," he answered her unasked question. "That is your horse he had just won his first race. We were more amazed than anything. It was the first time he proved that if we could only get him to start he would be a champion. I can have it copied for you –if you have not already enough photos of the boy." Natalie did not know what to say as it was really more a photo of Rob than Running Wind. Fortunately a loud beeping noise came from the kitchen and Rob slid off.

Satiated by the delicious baby leaf salad topped with warm goat's cheese followed by a rich boef bourguignon, Natalie sipped her wine and sat back in her chair. On the stereo Placcio Domingo was singing an aria from Verdi she felt relaxed and comfortable. The cat approached her yowling loudly. It squeezed it's deep blue eyes at her as if asking something, then leapt up onto her lap, purring loudly as she caressed its head.

Rob came in with strawberry compote with whipped cream and a bottle of champagne in a bucket of ice. He laid down the bucket and as he did so fished into his pocket. Natalie started with alarm –what was he doing champagne and – horrified she watched his hand as he laid a small box in front of her. Blinded by her panic Natalie did not even take in the shape of the box, the assumption she had jumped to appearing like reality to her. Rob was carefully opening the champagne bottle- so was not looking at his guest. Jumping up, thus throwing the cat un-ceremoniously to the floor Natalie suddenly insisted it was time for her to go and she did not want any dessert or wine. Her declaration was just too late; as the cork popped out making Rob reach for a glass as the fizzing liquid spurted over the rim. Bewildered Rob recovered well – thinking maybe she was un-well.

"Never mind I will call you a cab." Unwilling to remain in the room with Rob any longer, Natalie was unconsciously and un-characteristically rude.   "No I don't need any help; I will get one on my way."

"Natalie don't be silly Taxis hardly ever pass by here and it is past midnight."

 As she hesitated Rob picked up his phone pressed a few but-tons and ordered her a taxi. "You are in luck" He told her bitterly, "There is one in the neighbourhood it will be here in two minutes –that is- if you can bear two more minutes of my company."

Suddenly, Natalie got hold of her emotions and saw what a mess she had made of the evening. The untouched sweet and wine sitting on the table, she noticed that the offending box had vanished.

A car horn in the street sounded and Rob helped her on with her coat.

Rob said a curt goodbye as she left, his expression confused and pained. Picking up the affronted cat he sank heavily into the sofa. "God knows what I've done now Nero –I just don't understand this woman!"

Settling into the taxi Natalie gave her address; the trip was short as she searched for her purse, always at the bottom of her bag she mused, her hand caught on a small sharp edged object. The box – he had indeed given her the box.

In the quiet of her cottage Natalie sat down and opened the fateful box which she saw clearly now was a flat rectangle not as she had imagined a square cube, for a very long time she simply sat and stared into the box. Finally she had the courage to lift the object out into the light. Never had she been given such a beautiful present. Glistening in the light was an enamelled horses head, but not just any horse, it was unmistakably Running Wind. Only a true artist could have fashioned such an exquisite broach. Suddenly she felt lonely and foolish. *Oh I am just no good at relationships —I shall end up single all my life.*

The best and most beautiful things in the world cannot be seen or touched; they must be felt with the heart.
Hellen Keller

Chapter 11

Sue stood quiet and fascinated. The evening sun was just dropping below the distant hills on the horizon, reds and pinks swathed across the sky as if drawn by a painter's brush. A pair of doves swept across the paddock cooing softly and landed in the old apple tree on a gnarled old branch with its first spring flowers showing sparsely in white clusters. Natalie was working Running Wind by the last light of the day. The assignment she was working on was `flying changes of leg at the canter' for her Level 2 Quantum savvy qualification. She was riding her horse in a snaffle bridle with rope reins and an extra, long rope wrapped, cowboy style, round the horse's neck. As she cantered round the barrels Bill had placed in the arena, each time she changed direction she asked her horse to change his legs which he did fluently and easily.

When Sue had read the description of the assignment she knew Natalie would have some real problems with this impulsion test. *Canter a circle on a loose rein and show 2 simple lead changes through the middle.*

Make the circle bigger and gallop for 30 seconds; then spiral down to a smaller fast canter, circle and show 4 flying lead changes through the centre of the circle.
Come down to a halt and straight back up using the reins.

Natalie did not share her friend's worries. After all, hadn't she ridden Running Wind bareback with only the one rope when she saved him? She had also taken two horses to Level 1 in Quantum Savvy and Roxy to Level 2. Sue did not comment but what you can do in the heat of the moment with adrenalin flowing or riding fast in cold blood can be two different things. Also, Roxy was a lazy laid back horse whom Natalie had had to push. She knew Running Wind would be more difficult. Natalie's confidence, balance and spirit were about to be severely tested. If she got through this she would truly succeed in her dressage career, Sue believed.

For Natalie the homework for this assignment took several months. Often she would look to Bill for help, but he simply stood and watched. With great foresight Bill knew that Natalie had to come to terms with this part of the training herself. Not only was Bill never going to get on Running Wind himself, but also it was, he realized, very important that Natalie should achieve the special trust and connection needed for this test alone.

Natalie had done very little work with her horse using a bridle and although Bill helped her to put it on the first time, he thereafter refused to even help, remaining on the side lines or, even more alarming for Natalie, he sometimes was not even there at all. Only Bill knew what that cost him. Not only did he miss out on the pleasure of working with his boy, but also he was worried about the safety of Natalie.

Suddenly, all the fun and relaxed trusting times with her horse were turned upside down. Running Wind with a bit in his mouth was a completely different horse as his deeply in bred instinct to run fast came to the fore. Much to Natalie's horror when she first asked him to go faster he would speed up so quickly that she began to tense up and grip his sides, this resulted in him bucking; throwing his head down and arching his back. Several times Natalie nearly lost her balance completely, and once she actually fell off. Alarmed Natalie began to lose the confidence she had come to take for granted. The assignment called for her to be riding her horse in a large area, but at first she simply did not have enough confidence to canter, never mind gallop in the big field. Bill and Tom had created a smaller arena for her using white tape, but as this was not electrified Running Wind ran straight into the fence and then through it. Natalie clinging on; frightened for the first time realised that she was acting as the predator Shane and Meredith were always talking about. The precious trust she had always had in her horse was shattered. She was sacred and expecting her horse to trust her. Leadership and connection gone Running Wind no longer wanted to be with her and had no trust for her left at all. When she went out to the paddock to fetch her horse he would walk away and sometimes actually ran to the other side of the arena. More than once recently she had called for Bill to come and get the boy.

Her emotional fitness suffering badly it began to take more and more courage dredged from deep down to keep going and get back on her horse. Aware that her horse could in fact read her emotions, Natalie concentrated simply on being able to canter while controlling her breathing. Running Wind, himself worried and unforgiving, needed only to feel her nervousness or her body sitting wrongly or tense and he would bolt or buck to demonstrate his feelings that she should hold herself properly or get off !!

At night Natalie would lie awake, worried and afraid. Several times she actually asked herself if riding was for her, and whether she should give up and sell on Running Wind to a better rider. These feelings though strong did not fortunately last long as Natalie knew full well that her horse's unique character made selling him on a nearly impossible option. Also her love for her horse was so strong she really couldn't imagine life without him. If she was going to compete in proper dressage competitions she knew she would need to ride Running Wind in a bit and with a collected outline. Every day was filled with tears and fears, Natalie felt so helpless. She knew that it was vital she crack this with Running Wind. Although her work with Roxy had prepared her to a certain extent this was proving one of the toughest challenges of her life.

A call from another Quantum Savvy member, group organiser for Byfleet in Surrey Monica Andreewitch asking if Natalie wanted to join in on an Ultimate horse clinic she was arranging, was to be a life saver. Three of them were going to work with Meredith at the yard in Surrey and Natalie could join if she wished. This really was to be a benchmark time and Natalie who had felt recently the weight of struggling alone jumped at the chance. Sue immediately offered to drive the Toyota and tow the horse box for her. Natalie who had never found the necessary skill and courage to transport a horse was profoundly grateful to her best friend.

So long working alone apart from some help from Sue and Bill until recently had not prepared Natalie for the sheer joy of being part of a supportive group.

Natalie was thrilled to meet Monica whose long struggle with her difficult horse, Trooper, she had followed on the Quantum Savvy forum. When Natalie asked Monica about this she was completely candid, revealing her feelings at the time.

"He had rope phobia, rug phobia and being tied up phobia- and then there I was swinging ropes all around him, riding with long ropes and trying to throw ropes over his head. I almost gave up halfway through level 1 with him because it was never going to happen!!"

"Was he always like this?" Natalie asked mentally comparing him to Running Wind.

"I bought Trooper for my daughter. She was 15 at the time. It was a crazy thing to do as he had a history as a difficult horse. But he was completely different with her –he did everything for her. It was amazing; looking back I realise now they had a `special connection'. Paula has developed into a beautiful, very spiritual person. She was that then, but we didn't see it! Trooper did. When Paula gave him up for boys I got stuck with him desperately looking for that same connection. Trooper has taught me to keep my emotions down, my energy soft, be brave and patient with empathy, trust others in their knowledge and take advice, be able to let go of my ego and be humble."

All four woman involved were to look profoundly into their emotional mirrors and needed to dig very deep in their hearts for the courage and determination to achieve their goals. With insight and skill Meredith coached the best out of her pupils Natalie began for the first time in her life to understand herself; seeing her own faults and strengths echoed by her horse's reactions. Working with Monica, Brigitte and Rebecca, Natalie gave the gallop a run every day –just sheer speed. Laughing together, crying together the girls also rejoiced together. The nine days of the course seemed literally to fly by. Determined, committed and consistent Natalie began to build up her trust in Running Wind, and as she relaxed so too did her horse. The bolting and bucking stopped; her horse softened and started to actually look to his rider for the aid to stop. Connected to her and regaining his trust in her the horse was happier as Natalie no longer tensed and gripped mentally and physically. Running Wind freed of these ties began to feel comfortable and confident, finally leaving his deep rooted claustrophobia behind.

Elated by this success Natalie knew she was only half way through this task. Now she had to master the flying changes of legs, and then combine the two elements. Here Natalie realised that this was all about her position on the horse. The realisation that she often was guilty of unbalancing her horse came hard to Natalie who prided herself on her own balance. Trying too hard she actually caused her horse to trip up and once they both went down. Running Wind was forgiving. He let her remount and continue; time after time he coped with her lack of feel and bad timing. Working together like this with Natalie learning more about breathing, softness and consistency she felt her horse really begin to try for her and offer what she asked for.

The day she felt the first real fly change was a fantastic moment for Natalie. She was so focused on Running Wind's pace and leg position she felt the change immediately. A breakthrough of immense proportions had happened. Natalie felt she had been given something she did not even know she needed. Her immense pride in her horse and (if she admitted it herself) just bowled her over.

"The never ending assignment that's what I'll call it, Sue you have no idea how difficult it was." Natalie was reverently holding her blue string closely clutched in her hands–at last-- level 2 with Running Wind. Now Natalie had four of the precious trophies sent by Meredith a red Level 1 string with both Roxy and Running Wind and now a blue one with each horse.

Although she said nothing and simply nodded Sue knew exactly what Natalie was talking about. She had been witness to the tremendous learning curve Natalie had just undergone.

For every beauty there is an eye somewhere to see. For every truth there is an ear somewhere to hear. For every love there is a heart somewhere to receive it.
Ivan Panin

Chapter 12

Parking carefully, Rob noticed to his annoyance that Natalie's car was also there parked over by the hay barn. Sue greeted him cheerfully enough making a pot of tea for them both, but quickly got to the point.

"I hope you have come to see Natalie. She has not been herself these last few months. What on earth happened between you two? And don't prevaricate with me. She's not here at the moment so tell big sis all. "

"What do you mean not here? Her car is parked over by the barn."

"Oh, well, she must be out with her horse, I thought she said she was just giving Running Wind some hay then going. Anyway she is not here so tell all."

Rob described the events of the disastrous meal and his reaction.

"I guess she thought I was about to propose to her and over reacted, I have had time to think and of course it's obvious its Jeremy she wants to marry."

Sues guffaw of laughter at this was not what Rob was expecting. Affronted he complained. "No need to mock me Sue –of course she wants him. He's titled and much richer."

"Oh Rob, I am sorry. I didn't mean to offend you but look here in the Times."

Sue reached behind and took a paper cutting from the dresser she placed it carefully on the table in front of Rob. It was the announcement page from the Times Newspaper.

Slowly Rob read it, the full impact taking only a few seconds to sink in.

The engagement is announced between Lord Jeremy Philip Styles Castle son of the late Lord Charles John Styles Castle and Lady Alexandria Jane Castle of Woodstock House Oxfordshire and Katherine Chandler only daughter of Bertram Chandler and Angela Chandler of 3 Maidstone Gardens, Knightsbridge, London.

"Does Natalie know about this? How has she taken it?"

"Oh Rob of course she knows. She gave me the cutting, but Jeremy had told her a week before it appeared. I think he thought she might be upset but she was so pleased for him. She and Katherine are getting on so well and Natalie has asked Katherine to paint Running Wind for her."

"So she's not in love with Jeremy!" Rob looked elated.

"Indeed it was only Natalie being over reactive. She has not had a lucky time in love and is very sensitive. You will have to go slowly but I feel she really cares about you. Certainly she was very upset about how she behaved."

"Sue for the first time in my life I have met someone I would like to spend the rest of my life with. I promise I will have patience and not frighten her again."

"Well why not talk to her now? She's out riding Running Wind. That always puts her in a good mood. Just apologise and ask if you can be friends again. Then you can go as slowly as she needs."

"You're right Sue; I will ride out to meet her. Can I take Roxy?"

"Of course, she's in the small paddock. Take the old brown all purpose saddle. It fits her even better than the dressage one." As he hurried out she called after him. "Better ask Bill which way they went, but her favourite ride these days is over the long field and into the ancient forest there."

While Rob was giving Roxy a quick groom where the saddle would sit. Bill appeared.
"Do you know where Nat is? "
"She's gone over to them woods again." Bill replied shaking his head. "Goodness knows what she does there but she's been going there at least twice a week."
Rob carefully saddled and bridled Roxy and sprang jockey like into the saddle. Bill laughed as he watched Rob raise his stirrups, as he knew Tom had last used the saddle and he was 8 inches taller than Rob.

"Don't get her blown. She's getting older you know." Sue, looking out of her door, remonstrated her brother.

As if he had not heard Sue, Rob set off as if to win the Grand National, Roxy tossing her head at the unaccustomed speed she was being asked to give, but obediently galloping flat out across the stubble field.
From a distance the forest looked so thick and impenetrable as to be inaccessible. However, as he slowed Roxy at the edge of

the forest, he saw the small beaten track which led into the woods where there was a large enough gap to permit a horse and rider to pass easily. Having reached the woods, Rob realised he had no plan at all and was unsure what to say or do when he finally met with Natalie. Musing on this and trying out conversations in his head he nearly missed the sign that a horse had quit the path and taken an even smaller trail. The pile of horse droppings was a couple of yards to his left. Swinging Roxy down this track he was aware of the muffled sounds of Roxy's hooves and the quiet of the forest. He decided to slow down then stop and listen. At first he heard nothing then Roxy lifted her head, her ears pricked. He dismounted and slowly led the horse forward, some two hundred yards further on he saw light coming from another gap in the trees. He crept up to this gap and looked into a clearing which was almost a complete circle about one hundred yards across. Sitting in the centre of this space, the sun filtering in long low yellow slices from just above and back lighting her was Natalie. As dust motes floated round, she was bare foot and Running Wind was standing behind her. The horse's head was lowered to her shoulder and she held one hand on his nose. To Rob's left he saw a pair of Jodhpur boots and socks, Natalie's saddle and a long lead rope and a string halter lying on the ground. The naked horse and Natalie looked like one being, meditating in complete harmony. Roxy stood on a twig which snapped and Rob sank back hoping not to be seen. Running Wind lifted his head and cocked one ear in their direction. The spell broken Natalie stood and walked to her right, her horse followed her closely, she stopped and he stopped, then she swung back the other way Running Wind swung round, more animated this time. Natalie spun in a barefoot spiral her arms above her head and Running Wind spun too. She changed direction so did the horse. As Natalie stood up right on her points her equine partner reared and squealed. The pair continued to dance for a further 10 minutes. Rob held his breath in awe until he had to gasp and suck in a great breath of air. It was quite the most beautiful thing he had ever seen in his life, a graceful transcendental ballet. As Natalie quickened to her inner music so her horse followed her pace and rhythm perfectly. Rob felt waves of pure love for this exquisite dancer rush through his body. Suddenly as if to a hidden cue Natalie stopped and dropped in an elegant curtsy bowing her head, Rob watched amazed as Running Wind also dropped down with his head low. Natalie stood and walked slowly round her horse caressing him. She said not a word but to Rob it seemed as if the pair were speaking in a hidden language that only they could hear. Then Natalie gently slid over onto her horses back, he remained lying down until Natalie raised her arms. Slowly the big gelding rose. Natalie rode Running Wind round at a walk, trot and canter on both reins then she rode him into the centre and performed a stunning piaffe transitioning into a floating passage. Rob had no idea Natalie was capable of executing such advanced dressage work and on Running Wind bareback and bridleless, this amazed him.

Suddenly, the horse stopped and stood quite still as if by an unspoken and invisible cue from Natalie.

"Well, Rob. Why don't you say hello. "Natalie's tone was teasing.

Uncertainly Rob approached until he could be seen. "How did you know it was me?" he asked incredulous.

"Easy "Natalie replied. "Running Wind heard you –he gave a small welcome horse wicker which I guess you did not hear. It told me a horse he knew and liked, Roxy, his special buddy was here ridden by someone he knew and liked. Well his favourite two people apart from me are you and Bill. Bill would never ride Roxy here so I knew it was you all along."

"You mean you performed that dance for me?"

"Of course. Who else?" As she spoke Natalie had been tacking up her horse and made her one long rope into two reins by tying it under Running Wind's nose. With great agility she hopped on her horse and headed out of the forest. Rob taking her lead sprang onto Roxy and followed her along the path and out of the forest.

The sun was very near to the ground giving a deep reddish glow to the stubble field. Rob just behind Natalie was suddenly filled with devilish mischief. Quietly he raised his stirrups a couple of holes then digging his heels into Roxy's flanks he sped passed Natalie, hunched over Roxy's withers crying "Race you to the stables."

Taken a bit by surprise Natalie saw Roxy move fast away, then laughing she leant forwards and whispered into Running Wind's ears "Go Toady go."

Natalie was not prepared for the immediate surge forwards her horse performed. In all her riding and training- even the impulsion assignment Natalie had never ridden Running Wind at such a speed, but she soon was overtaken with adrenalin and excitement in this new sensation. She had such total trust in her horse that she just sat and let him run. Poor over weight Roxy the 16.2hh Hanoverian cross was simply no match for the fit, sleek 16.3hh ex racing thoroughbred and about halfway up the long field Natalie passed Rob carelessly blowing him a kiss as she left him behind.

Natalie waited for Rob to appear on Roxy who was wheezing as they cantered slowly up. She had dismounted and loosened the girth; Running Wind looked as ever as if he could have easily repeated the whole evening.

"You win, Natalie." Rob said admiringly.

"We were a little mismatched." Natalie confessed a huge grin on her face.

"Natalie I'm sorry I upset you. I truly did not mean to." Rob's face was serious. He slowly dismounted and walked towards Natalie.

"Rob I'm sorry too, I over reacted and hurt you, and I never thanked you for your beautiful present, I just love it." As she said this she leant towards Rob, impulsively he caught her in his arms and kissed her lightly on the lips. Setting her free before she felt pressured.

Looking out of the window Sue commented to Tom sardonically, "The young lovers seem to have patched up their differences, but don't count on Roxy for lessons for a couple of days, I'll give that brother of mine what for."

"Oh Sue, give them a break, this yard has been so much better in all ways since Natalie arrived. Bill is just the best lad we have ever had, calm hardworking and a good influence on the other lads. And let's face it since you started with Quantum Savvy all the horses have been easier to work on the ground and much better behaved under saddle."

As a result of the appropriate gymnastics and training of the horse. The appearance and the movements of the horse will be more beautiful. *Alois Podhajsky (The complete training of horse and rider1965)*

Chapter 13

"Time now." Sue said, "For you to do some real training – as you continue to work on your level 3 with Quantum Savvy you need a better trainer than me."

Natalie was about to protest at this, but one look at Sue's face stopped her.

"It is time you took lessons with Tom." In all the time Natalie had been riding at their yard she had only rarely watched Tom give a lesson never mind thought of him giving her coaching. A busy competitor in national and international competitions Tom was, it seemed, nearly always busy.

"Don't worry Natalie." Sue laughed at her friend's face. "Not only does he not bite –well not often- but it was his idea. Laura Penglington has moved to Brighton so he can take on a new pupil."

The first sound Natalie heard as they entered the indoor school was the soft thudding of a horse's hooves cantering gently round. The music was from a ballet Natalie had once performed and she was at once extremely interested. From the gallery they looked down upon a slim elegant young woman on a huge black stallion; the smell of heated horse was intoxicating for Natalie as she watched the supreme skill of the rider.

Tom was standing in the middle of the school and he spoke suddenly encouragingly. "You need to put your horse in the place where he can say *no problem* and let the dance begin. To get more energy and poise into the trot. Timing is everything." He looked up at the rider as he spoke "Come on let's hear the music." The rider slowed to a lovely balanced trot and as she encouraged her horse into a higher elevation she made a seemingly effortless transition into a stylish floating passage.

Natalie realised that she had reached a crossroads –probably one of the most important of her life. This was it --not only the best trainer she could possibly have, but also the real start of her dressage career.

Continuing with her Quantum Savvy and still being expertly coached by Meredith blended so well with Tom's style of dressage training. Just as his wife had been, Tom was impressed by how supple laterally Natalie's horse was and how he followed her seat. That Natalie was a very talented and hard working rider pleased Tom. At last he had a worthy pupil. Well she was going to need all her dedication and strength both mental and physical. Tom had only one way of looking at competing at dressage --- winning.

Sue turned back to the sink as Tom sank his lean, tall form heavily into his favourite chair in the kitchen, pretending to be washing vegetables although they were all clean. She waited for him to begin.

With a sigh Tom pushed his hair back and finally spoke, "God Sue. Natalie really is such a trial; she just won't believe me that she is more than ready to compete at Grand Prix level. I don't know what's stopping her. I'm sure it's not a lack of confidence in herself or her horse. You should see the connection she gets with Running Wind. I've taught many riders but she is just special but just won't hear it she's even better than I will ever be, but it's been two years now since she was ready. What can I do to get her to a top competition?"

"Leave it with me Tom. I think I can persuade her."

Sue followed Natalie into her kitchen and watched as she carefully opened the bottle of wine she had brought. Drops of condensation ran down the yellow bottle. Pouring generously Natalie filled the two large glasses.

Leaning back against her cooker Natalie took a small sip of the delicious cool, white wine and asked her friend." Well what are we celebrating?"

Taking the opening given to her Sue raised her glass and replied, "To your boy winning his first major competition."

"What?" Natalie frowned at Sue. "I haven't entered any competitions ----have I?" she added as Sue coloured slightly.

"Well actually, I-hum-well, I have um… entered you for a Championship Competition."

Natalie stared furiously at Sue.

"Don't give me that look Natalie –just tell me. Is my husband wasting all these hours of lessons for nothing not to say all the effort your horse is putting in? Its time you showed the world what you can both achieve. In fact, you owe it to us all, Running Wind, Bill, Rob, Tom and actually me as well.

Natalie took another taste of her wine and looked down.

"Are you accusing me of being selfish?" My very best friend turning against me! Colour was spreading up Natalie's neck and her voice was shrill.

"No Natalie don't be silly. Of course I am not turning away from you, but yes you are being a little self interested when you refuse to listen to Tom when he says you are more than ready to compete. What's stopping you? Surely you are not afraid of failing."

"Afraid! No I certainly am not, I just -well I am not sure my performance will be perfect enough, and I have no ideas about the choreography."

"Oh Natalie!" Sue encouraged her friend. "Now you have your level 3 Quantum savvy and are working on level 4 it is time. Tom says you will get 10 in all your transitions from Running Wind's marvellous passage to piaffe and as for artistic impression- you and Running Wind look like one being as if you were dancing again- through your horse's legs."

Pleased at this compliment Natalie swallowed not only another sip of her wine, but also her pride and uncertainty "OK Sue you win ---so which competition have I entered? "

"That's more like it". Sue kept her voice even but she was exultant inside, *oh ho Tom will be so happy.* "Well- I've entered you in the Grand Prix class at Oldencraig in three weeks time."

Natalie wasn't sure whether to be excited or alarmed at this – three weeks! So she had to do some work on the extended walk now. Her main thought though was the choreography for the freestyle to music. She needed help with this but to whom could she turn. Suddenly she had an idea –but of course who else?

The music sounded glorious booming from the speakers. Isobel watched as Natalie ran through the compulsive elements for her grand prix test. The phone call from her favourite ever pupil, which came out of the blue, had surprised her but when she had time to reflect upon what it meant she was not only delighted to help but fired with enthusiasm and ideas. The sight of the huge and powerful horse dancing with tiny Natalie on his back brought to mind images from the *Jungle Book.* The bear and the boy; yes the `Bear Necessities' but could they use it? Isobel could spare only two days from her busy schedule so they had a lot of work to do. Grey haired and well over 50 she was nonetheless a seemingly everlastingly elegant and dignified lady. Her work ethics had not changed either and she was set to put Natalie through a couple of days of really hard travail.

Irrespective of her age Isobel had a very open mind about the choice of music for the test. Natalie had expected her teacher to pick only music from ballets or certainly classical music so Isobel's first choice was a complete surprise to both Natalie and Tom who was in on their sessions. "Right Natalie. I think this music is perfect for that beautiful elevated trot -called `passage' I believe." *Addicted to Love* by Robert Palmer was indeed a great beat and Natalie found it easy to practise passage to this track Running Wind's ears pricked, his elevation was superb and graceful. It looked so easy.

"Can you do a pirouette in this trot now, Natalie." Isobel's voice was strong and commanding Tom was very impressed with her. *She must have done some serious reading about dressage, she seems so knowledgeable.*

In her state of heightened excitement Natalie thought she had arrived in paradise when she saw the beautiful grounds and buildings with flowers everywhere and a lovely lake. Oldencraig was everything she had been told it was. Such an elite venue for her first Grand Prix competition. Tom drove between the lovely wrought iron gates in black and gold to the immaculate stables and barn. As Bill led the boy off to be stabled Natalie took in the surroundings and fabulous facilities. She laughed to her self when she saw the Jacuzzi. *Ha Rob will want to try that one out when he arrives this evening.*

Marion Shellwood reached her arm over the starched white table cloth avoiding the pretty flowers in a crystal vase and grabbed the water bottle. As she filled her glass she turned to her scribe, making sure she was ready. To her left Henri Duchamp was muttering to himself *"Alors, la petite belle ballerine sur son cheval du course"* Although Marion knew she should refrain from any preferences or indeed any personalisations, she had to agree with Henri. Her interest in the diminutive dancer and her impressive horse had been fired up during her performance yesterday. At the moment she was actually in equal first place with one of the world's top riders, Frederica Von Sheulburg. This was a stunning achievement; where had this talented rider and her so expressive horse been hiding. To come out of no where and be so high was amazing. Marion had to admit to herself she really was looking forward to this `Freestyle to Music' presentation.

His hooves tapping in complete rhythm to the beat of the music as they entered in Passage. Natalie brought her horse to a perfectly square halt with her horse following her very thoughts as her aid for this halt was so tiny as to be invisible.

The most striking thing about this horse thought Marion *was the expression on his face calm, happy and trusting the contentment echoed in his whole body, tail held high swinging softly from side to side in rhythm with his trot.* The horse and rider set off after the salute in a wonderful floating passage which blended easily into a superb piaffe. The music changed to *Dancing Queen* by Abba and Natalie achieved a perfect transition from trot to canter with no hesitation. As she watched Marion did not miss the trust between horse and rider as Running Wind covered the ground with a huge extended canter easily coming back to a canter pirouette.

Back to passage to the music from the Jungle book *The Bear Necessities* Running Wind danced his way to the judge at corner

H setting off in a half pass in passage. As he flowed effortlessly across the arena his outside leg was stepping right across.

Marion's full attention was on the pair as she watched closely- yes indeed she had seen right. Now they were close and about to pass in front of her she was sure of the hint of slackness in the reins so seldom seen in dressage competitions, showing the horse going forwards into the contact. It looked so beautiful as Running Wind lifted in his withers to allow greater collection and vertical flexion. The horse going to comfort and not away from pressure.

In the 12 flying changes Natalie could feel how straight her horse was. Grinning inwardly she thought of all the time spent on getting the perfect hind quarter yield. *"Thanks Meredith."*

This combination were technically as good as Fredericka Von Sheulburg and Monotony Dimple, but Marion had never seen such artistic impression. Even before the finale where Natalie trotted up holding the reins in one hand and halted faultlessly. Marion knew she was going to give top marks. She watched closely as her scribe wrote 93% on the paper.

Three other judges had the same thoughts as Marion and Natalie's final score was 87%. A spectacular debut in Grand Prix.

The horse felt it; like the snap of a twig.
Something silken fell away,
The umbilical of his life was gone.
Should he too fly?
No, another force still held him tethered to the ground.

Avril Wilson (The Healing Touch)

Chapter 14

The smell of new mown grass was intoxicating as Natalie worked in her garden. She had recently turned over some of her lawn to create a fragrant and useful culinary herb garden. When she heard the ringing doorbell she rose, removing her gloves and ran indoors to the front door. Rob stood there his face very grave. Natalie knew at once that it was bad news. Her heart plummeted as all kinds of imagined scenarios rushed into her mind. "Running Wind?" she cried.

"Running Wind is fine Natalie. I am afraid it is Bill. Oh, Natalie, there is no easy way to tell you this; he had a massive stroke early this morning and died in the ambulance."

"No-- not Bill!" Natalie sank to her knees. Although he had recently celebrated his 74th birthday she had always thought he would go on forever. Over the last 7 years she and Bill had become very close. He had seemed to her a gentle father figure and, of course, they shared the same deep love for Running Wind.

Gently Rob helped her up and held her close as she wept. Finally Rob steered her into the kitchen where he boiled the kettle and made her a cup of very strong sweet tea. He would have liked to put a shot of Brandy or Whisky in, but he knew Natalie hardly ever drank and never had spirits in the house.

"He has no family apart from us, has he? " Still tearful Natalie questioned Rob.

"I never heard him speak of any and no one but me visited him when he was in hospital after the crash."

"Well, then, it is up to us to give him a proper send off."

Natalie sat looking pensive for some time; grateful that Rob did not speak and was leaving her to her thoughts.

"I think we should hire a horse drawn hearse. You know one of those antique glass sided ones with a pair of black horses."

"Natalie that is a great idea, Bill's only true love in life was horses."

Later that day Natalie drove to the stables. Sue met her as she parked.

"I am so sorry,Natalie, we all thought a lot of Bill he was the hardest working lad we ever had here. "

"How's Running Wind? This must be the first morning for 7 years Bill has not fed his boy. "

"I fed him but he did not touch his bucket. Frankly I am glad you are here he seems very depressed."

Natalie went straight to her horse. He nickered at her when she entered his stable. As she took him to the small home paddock where there was some early spring grass she started to talk to him. Reminded of the day she had told him her life history Natalie released her horse and sat on the grass to watch him. Normally he would have walked off cropping and chomping. He remained at her side nibbling a little around her. Running Wind had come over to her blowing down his nose as she held out her hand, she sat cross-legged and he dropped his nose into her hands. This was always their special moment when their two souls seemed to combine as one. Natalie talked of Bill, what he Running Wind meant to Bill and how sorry she was they would not all be together any more. For Natalie one of the saddest things was that she had not yet told Bill that she was probably going to be selected to ride Running Wind in the 2016 Olympics in Freestyle Dressage. Tom had told her a few days ago but cautioned her not to mention it to anyone in case she was not selected. "He would have been so proud of you 'Toady' we will just have to do our best without him. He would have expected nothing less."

Jeremy closed the door to his office "Natalie, I am so sorry. We all liked and admired Bill, but you were the closest to him. Please sit down I have some news for you."

Natalie sat elegantly in the chair; Jeremy thought she had never looked more beautiful or sad.

"You know I am executor of his will," Jeremy continued. "Bill has only one benefactor in his will. Natalie he has left all his money to you. There is actually quite a lot as he rarely spent any money and never gambled after Running Wind fell. He bet quite a lot of money when Running Wind was racing though, always on his boy to win and amassed £35 000. He would not touch this money. One day I asked him why and he told me he wanted to be ready just in case you ever sold Running Wind. In later years I think he realised you would never sell your horse but he still wouldn't touch his savings.

"His help especially in the early years was invaluable I didn't realise he had so much money stashed away. I think the only things he spent his money on apart from a few pints down at the pub were horse treats, herbal feeds, and shampoos etc for Running Wind. I always told him to give me the receipts and I would pay for them but he just wanted to give his boy something."

"The funeral will be on Wednesday at 11.00," Natalie informed Jeremy.

"I want to do something special for him Jeremy and I have a question to ask." Natalie looked up and met Jeremy's eyes. He was touched by the profound sentiment in her gaze.

"I have arranged a horse drawn hearse for the funeral, but I also want something more for Bill. I spoke with Phillip Fuller director of the firm who are bringing the hearse and he sees no reason why not. I would like Running Wind to follow behind the hearse, Rob has agreed to ride him--- and I would love him to wear your racing colours."

"My dear Natalie, what a charming idea. Of course Rob can wear my colours and please allow me to hire a Landau to take all the rest of us. I guess Sue and her family will come."

Since his marriage to Kate Jeremy had become one of her closest friends. When finally he had accepted that she would never marry him he had switched to being like an older brother and looked after her.

It was arranged that Natalie, Jeremy, Kate, Sue, Ellie and Tom would all follow in the Landau and the rest of Jeremy's family, and Melanie would be in a vintage black Rolls behind.

Natalie was just finishing pleating a black ribbon into Running Wind's mane when Rob arrived. As he watched her put in the last stitch and leave the end of the ribbon trailing, he felt a surge of love for them both. The dainty beautiful but hardworking and determined Natalie and the magnificent elegant horse who had not only been transformed by her but had also healed her.

Although had been only 6 days since Bills death Natalie had spent nearly every waking moment with her horse. They had all been afraid that without Bill Running Wind might have re-lapsed into his old behaviour. The day following the tragic news Sue watched wistfully as Natalie rode her horse across the long field and entered at her special spot. Rob had described to his sister in detail what he had seen Natalie doing with her horse in the clearing. Sue respected Natalie especially at this time of grieving but she fervently wished she, too, could just for once see Natalie and Running Wind dancing free. Tom joined his wife at the window and put his arm round her shoulders. He knew what she was thinking. Natalie disappeared into the woods. "Well, we needn't have worried anyway." Tom ob-served. "Running Wind is fine now."

"As long as Natalie is around, or Rob. He still doesn't really settle with anyone else."

Sue turned away from the window –she put the kettle on the Aga and reached for cups. The rich smell of baking drifted round the kitchen as Sue removed a ginger-bread from the Aga. Fifteen minutes later Tom was still standing looking out over the long field, a second cup of tea in his hand as Sue cleared the plates into the sink.

"Quick, Sue, look."

Sue hurried back to the window. In the growing dusk she saw two figures, ghost-like, lit by the thin light of the rising moon. An ethereal luminosity surrounded them. As they came closer you could see that the horse was walking free. Natalie held his halter and lead rope in her left hand and the horse walked on her right shoulder. Their pace was perfectly matched. There was something eerily spiritual about the scene. Sue realised that the way she looked at training and working with her horses had changed so much since Natalie came. The yard would never be the same again, but who would want to change the wonderful atmosphere and the calm willing horses?

The church was only 3 miles from Sue's Yard, so the funeral firm parked their lorry there and hitched up their horses to the hearse. After two days of rain the sun had finally come out and everything looked and smelt wonderfully fresh. Wearing a black suit and pillbox hat with a veil Natalie watched the two magnificent Friesians being prepared. Their coats were every bit as shiny as Running Wind's –Natalie had groomed him as if for a competition. Their bridles and the breast plates gleaming with highly polished brasses. As they moved their heads the Red plumes on the top of their bridles waved elegantly. The procession was ready with Bill's coffin in the glass-sided hearse. Rob took up his place behind on a prancing Running Wind. More hooves sounded as the Landau came round into the yard pulled by four matching bay horses closely followed by the vintage Rolls. Natalie stepped into the carriage and as if by a signal they started slowly out of the yard and over the stone bridge.

The entourage attracted quite a crowd as they walked in slow procession to the church. Two solemn pall bearers walked in front of the hearse then Running Wind on his toes, the Black ribbon on his mane streaming behind him. From the Landau Natalie watched the, man she now knew she loved more than ever ride the horse she loved so much who had been responsible for bringing them together.

As Bill was laid in the ground Graham Locking national chaplain to horse racing gave an eloquent speech and Rob added a eulogy of his own, hot wet tears streamed down Natalie's face. Clods of earth were thrown onto the coffin and Running Wind who was being held by the coach driver let out a huge whinny. Although Natalie realised it was only because

172

both she and Rob were out of his sight, she felt it was a last fitting epitaph from the horse.

Where in this wide world can man find nobil-
ity without pride, friendship without envy or
beauty without vanity?
Here where grace is served with muscle and
strength by gentleness confined. He serves
without servility, he has fought without en-
mity.
There is nothing so powerful, nothing less
violent, nothing so quick, nothing more po-
tent.
Ronald Duncan (The Horse 1954)

Chapter 15

Snow crunched beneath her boots; ice crystals sparkling like
miniature diamonds in the glow under the yard lights. It was
6.00 in the morning. Natalie shivered as she picked up a bucket
from the pile just inside the tack room. Tom's voice echoed
round the yard as he fed the other horses. Since Bill's death
Running Wind would hardly touch a bucket from anyone but
Natalie or Rob. Natalie made a great effort to be there for the
boy, now her sole charge. Carefully the feed was mixed with
water from a container as the taps were all frozen. Running
Wind's box was diagonally across from the tack room. Melted
snow had turned to ice overnight and the yard was lethal.
Struggling to keep her balance Natalie opened the top door to a
welcome wicker, her horse snuffling in the bucket before she

could place it down for him. Turning out Running Wind Natalie was as always grateful to the Quantum Savvy ground-work as her horse was calm, gentle, respectful and a pleasure to handle even in these difficult conditions. Returning to the tack room Natalie filled a large water bucket and sloshed across the yard once more, passing a grim faced Tom and Andy, his current lad, both also struggling to carry water. Carefully she re crossed the slippery ice to fill the hay net in the big hay barn. As she cut open a new fresh smelling bale Sue appeared carrying two nets.

"Are you sure about this Natalie? With this severe weather can you really cope alone?" Sue turned a worried expression on her face, to Natalie, as they both forced hay into the nets.

"Please, Sue, don't worry Ellie will be back from her dance rehearsal at 4.30" Natalie reassured her friend. "And you, Tom, Andy and Jenny will return at 6.00. I know how much this competition means to you both."

"But to manage all alone in this weather – promise me you will be careful especially bringing in the young colt –he's a bit of a wilful devil. Maybe wait until Ellie comes back to help you." But even as she said this Sue knew that a 14 month old colt could not be left out so long in the cold; and more snow was forecast. "It is only at times like this that we realise just how invaluable Bill was. He was rarely not here, only when he went with you and his boy to a competition. He never complained and all the horses were so good with him. He really had a gift with them. This new lad James will not be with us long I fear. This is the second time he has called in sick in a month and always on a Saturday. When we employed him, we made it plain he would always be needed on a Saturday because of the dressage competitions; I think he spends his Friday nights in the pub which is no help to us."

"I'll be fine Sue. Off you go and make sure you come back with that Championship Cup."

Watching the lorry leave Natalie shuddered, certain that it was only the cold not some terrible premonition she wheeled the laden barrow to the muck heap. Deciding to have an early lunch as soon as all the stables were prepared Natalie emptied the barrow on the steaming pile. As she worked, she thought about Cold Blackberry aka Berry the young Hanoverian colt Sue was worried about. Although only 14 months old, he was already 15 hands high and very full of himself. Tom loved his character and the colt certainly behaved better with Tom than anyone else, but Natalie knew Bill would have been more connected with the colt and would have had him better under control. "A good dressage horse needs confidence and expression in his character." Natalie wryly remembered Tom's words on a recent occasion when Berry had kicked Andy.

Natalie decided to bring in Roxy first then Running Wind and Berry last. The colt was wont to wind up when he went past other horses in the field, causing Running Wind to charge up and down his paddock, something Natalie wished to avoid with so much ice on the ground.

Roxy was waiting impatiently by the field gate. Always one for her comforts she was eager for her warm stable and hay net. The big gentle horse plodded slowly and prudently across the yard and needed no encouragement to enter her stable. For once Natalie did not use Bill's special whistle to call her boy fearing for his legs on the slush. In the event he was not far from his gate and came slowly over as soon as he saw her.

Leaving Roxy and Running Wind rugged and happily munching their hay, Natalie then had only Berry to bring in, all the other horses having gone to the competition in which Tom and his pupil Jennifer Marsh were competing.

As the radio weather forecast had predicted; it had started snowing again. Huge light flakes showering down. Natalie could have stood and admired them, even found them pretty if not for all she still had to do.

Checking that Berry's stable had plenty of water and hay ready she set off towards his paddock. Oblivious of the snow and muddy slush Berry was happily trotting up to the gate when he heard her. The big chestnut colt was an impressive horse. He was crowding the gate as Natalie opened it so she swung the leather end of her rope in his direction. Seeing the swinging rope Berry respectfully kept his distance. The ground was very slippery and hardened mud and ice was rucked into ridges and big holes. Berry politely let Natalie put on the string halter. Relieved that he did not play her up with the ground so treacherous Natalie opened the gate. At this Berry decided to rush through the gate. Just outside of the gate was a large puddle which was completely frozen. Berry hit this puddle in his haste, pulling on the rope Natalie held, his hooves went entirely from under him and he crashed to the ground. As he fell his legs went sideways swiping at Natalie bringing her down against the gate post. Natalie gasped in pain as she heard a cracking sound. Berry struggled frantically, his instinct told him he was vulnerable and he had to get up. Aware that she had sustained some damage Natalie now feared worse as the horse finally forced himself up right, in doing so his right front hoof stood firmly on her collar bone. Another rush of pain went through her body. To her horror she realised that she no longer held the rope. Shaken by his fall Berry stood immobile; his hoof still pinning Natalie down. Drawing on all her reserves Natalie remembered the first time she ever stood up on her points. *I must endure this* she thought, *if I cry out or try to move I could spook him in to running off maybe falling again and damaging his legs.* The constant fear of all horse owners especially Natalie, is that their horse should damage, or worse break, one of their legs. Natalie lay totally motionless feeling the cold creeping through her clothes from the ice and the agony in her body. That both her collar bone and at least one bone in her ribs were broken she was sure. Her only thought was to keep Berry safe and avoid any more injury to her self. It would be more than an hour before Ellie came back `always assuming' she would return on time –at 18 she was often side-tracked on the way or went for a coffee with her mates. The large snow flakes were melting as they fell on her face but were also clogging up her eyes. She had to get up soon; her body was stiffening and it was dangerous in these conditions to remain lying on the ground. How to do so without upsetting Berry and sending him rushing across the yard. She knew he would head straight for Running Winds box to challenge him over the door, although only a game he had already bitten her boy on his lip. Slowly, so very slowly, Natalie reached up and touched Berry's hoof which was so heavy on her chest. The horse snorted and looked down. With gentle rhythmic motion Natalie started caressing the horse from his hoof to his hock, very aware of the agony not only from her left collar bone but also her back where she was sure she must have also sustained some serious damage. Although she desperately wanted to move, she steeled herself, prepared to continue reassuring the colt as long as necessary. It seemed forever before Natalie was confident enough to lightly lift the hoof. New pain surged through her as she held the hoof an inch or two from her face. Berry snorted again. Then to her lasting relief shifted sideways with his front, placing his hoof next to her head. The reprieve was short lived when she realised that as Berry was now standing on her hair she was still pinned to the ground. Her head was desperately cold, her hair soaking wet. Although she had warm leggings on under her jodhpurs the icy damp was penetrating through, chilling her even more. *Soon* she thought, shaking, *I will not be able to stand.* Berry snorted again Natalie looked up at him through the snow. He was also shivering his thin turnout rug which was not enough to keep out this severe chill was covered in a thick white layer. The rope Natalie noticed was still attached to the string halter hanging by its brass snap straight down from the horse's chin. With hope

Natalie realised the rope then lay not far from her. Gradually inching her arm out, she felt for the rope, her frozen fingers stiff and unresponsive, the pain in them had been overshadowed by her fear for the horse and her injuries. The snow was still falling heavily. Lying on the ice and melted snow from two days ago. The sky was dusky, dark grey and the temperature plummeting. She simply had to get up. Straining with every muscle in her arm forcing her fingers to work, at last she touched the rope. Inch by inch she moved. Waves of tormenting pain came with each effort. Eventually, she had the end of the rope; gradually she started shaking the rope- just a tiny wiggle at first, then adding a little more pressure. Then, oh miracle Berry responded with a slight shift backwards of his weight. Instantly rewarding this miniscule try Natalie let the rope fall quiet. When a few more minutes had passed Natalie resumed the light shake again. This time the horse took a couple of backwards steps. It was enough! Her hair freed she could now very cautiously move. The pain in her back was like a knife penetrating but she knew she really had to get into the warmth and get Berry warm too.

Only after a long terrible struggle did Natalie manage to get onto her knees. Freezing icy drips ran down inside her clothes making her shiver again. Berry tensed as she rose, but Natalie talked gently to him and caressed him in round massaging strokes. Unable to stand up-right properly Natalie walked bent over with Berry to his stable, unhurriedly and cautiously; step by agonizing step with the colt quiet and subdued. Philosophically she thought that if she had to break a collar bone that it was at least her left. She kept her left arm across her chest holding her jacket. Feeling a bit nauseous and dizzy, Natalie was keen to stable and rug the young colt afraid she might collapse.

Totally unaware of the pain and problems he had caused for Natalie Berry was nonchalantly snatching at his hay net as she forced herself through the pain and disability of only using one arm to change his rugs.

It was not far across the yard to the house, but Natalie felt she really just could not face it. Her head swimming she opened the door of the box next to Berry's. An animal shifted over as she came in as if to make room, leaning heavily on the top of the door she just managed to close the bottom part.

"Nat! NAT! NATALIE!" Elle's voice became shrill as she began to panic. When she had not found Natalie waiting in the house for her, Ellie had looked first in the tack room, then the hay barn. Where was she? As her eyes scanned the yard she noticed that Running Wind's top door was open and despite her frantic shouting there was no sign of the horse. Knowing that most horses would have looked out as she yelled Ellie made her way to the box. When she looked over the top she just couldn't believe it. Natalie was lying face down in the straw and manure, her clothes wet and dirty she was not moving. The most amazing thing was that Running Wind was lying right next to her his whole right side in contact with her body. He did not move even when he saw Ellie, though he did give a small nicker.

"You know Natalie; the doctors said Running Wind most probably saved your life. The warmth from his body meant the hypothermia you suffered from was not fatal." Sue drove into the driveway carefully in the snow ruts. The hospital had kept Natalie in overnight as she was in the first throws of serious hyperthermia; she was to stay with Sue and Tom for at least a week.

"I know, Sue. Apparently I was so wet and it was so cold they were amazed I was alive. How fitting now my boy has saved me. At least they agreed to put on this clavicle brace. I could not have done much with a sling on. It is a bit like being in a straight jacket but it really does help to be able to use both arms."

Sue marvelled at her friend's stoicism she never complained of pain, just not being able to work and ride her horse.

"Leave that Natalie, Andy will bring it for you," Tom's voice was commanding." Take him his bucket. We'll do the water and hay." It was just two weeks since Natalie's fall and she was very obviously still in pain. Further snowfalls meant that the roads were still treacherous and Natalie could not drive herself any-way. As Running Wind would not happily take his feed from anyone else, it made sense for Natalie to remain with her friends. Ellie was delighted and Sue constantly clucked round her like a mother hen. All this attention was a little claustropho-bic for the independent Natalie as Rob had also been visiting as often as his race commitments and the road conditions would allow. Rob's respect and love for Running Wind had deepened when he was told how the horse had saved Natalie.

Standing in the tribune and looking down on Natalie and her magnificent horse Tom saw the dedication this young woman had. *No wonder she was a great ballerina. It's only a bare month since Berry broke her collar bone and rib; Sue only took her clavicle rings off yesterday.* Sue had been helping Natalie to remove and replace this brace whenever she wanted to shower so he knew how painful this operation was.

"I feel like my arm is very heavy," was all she said and here she was riding Running Wind in a light string halter with one long rope held in her right hand. Her stirrups were crossed in front of the saddle and she was sitting easily to the trot without them. Amazed, Tom watched her change the rein on the diago-nal by throwing her one rope over Running Winds head again just using her right hand. Unconcerned by this rope flying past his eyes the horse carried on in his perfect rhythm. When Nata-lie had told him she needed to work on her seat after a month out of the saddle he had not imagined this. The only help she would take was letting Tom lift the saddle onto her horse's back. Running Wind himself had helped her put the halter on. Not only had he dropped his head really low for her but he had turned completely to her in a full flex and held his head absolutely still. Holding one end of the halter in her left hand her right did all the work passing the loop over his nose then bringing the long end round and tying the knot. As Tom watched Natalie brought her horse in a perfect squared halt.

"Can you please bring me my black savvy string. It's on my stick up there I think, up against a chair."

Tom took the 6'string down, and gave it to Natalie. "Thanks, Tom" she said as she attached the string round her horse's neck "Here." she handed him the end of her long rope and lent forwards to undo the halter. Tom gently slipped the halter off Running Wind. This was the side of Natalie's riding which most impressed Tom. She was capable of riding not only without a bit but also with no rope. In fact he knew that the savvy string was only there as a back up and that she would ride her horse with her body. Having only recently tried riding Black Isle his Grand Prix horse with just the halter and no bit he had done so with the rope tied under his horse's nose making two reins, he had yet to try it with just one rope. It was beyond his imagination to think of riding the powerful black stallion with just a string round his neck.

With the Olympics only 7 months away Natalie was right. She not only had to keep her horse fit but also regain her own strength while practising all the moves.

Her feet back in her stirrups Tom called to her "OK, Natalie, let's see that half pass in passage again." Never tiring from watching how Natalie achieved such collection without the reins, Tom could but marvel at the true connection between horse and rider. In the beginning Running wind had been somewhat one sided and Tom had stressed the importance of balancing the work on both sides in order to get good bends from fluent equilibrium. Natalie was, Tom realized, a real performer *she will go in and show off in complete harmony with her horse*. As horse and rider crossed the school in a naturally flowing passage Tom thought about the amazing chance his pupil had been given. To ride in the Olympics! That she really deserved it he did not doubt, but what an incredible life this horse and rider had already lived through. *Could they* he asked himself *actually win a medal?*

Finally the heavy rain shower had stopped. Big fluffy cumulus clouds scudded across the sky. Natalie was relieved to be working in the out door school again and she knew her horse was also glad of the fresh air even if it was in fact very fresh. The pair would much rather be out in the cold than inside. Early April was a delightful time with the smell of the spring in the air of blossoms and grass. A cuckoo sounded from the woods, making Natalie smile.

"Right, let's see that extended trot. I want you to make the steps bigger and slower. Get that special front elevation he does so well." Tom watched as the horse performed a very active extended trot really covering the ground. "That's it, Natalie, come on get brave –he is still a little bit big behind, We need his front legs a little lower –good- balance girl, balance, excellent.... much better balance and push feel the hindquarters swing. That's it superb." Tom meant it. When Running Wind was fully flowing his extended trot really was extraordinary."If you can get him moving like this a medal will be yours." A big regret in the Mobley household was the fact that none of them would be able to go to Rio de Janero. Not only was it too far but they all had commitments. Ellie was due to star in a local theatrical performance which of course her parents wanted to attend. Tom's pupil also had an important Advanced Médium Affiliated competition so they were all tied to the yard. Rob, however was going he had worked his racing schedule round the trip which he and Natalaie had been planning for months.

My horse's feet are as swift as rolling thunder
He carries me away from all my fears
And when the world threatens to fall asunder
His mane is there to wipe away my fears
Bonnie Lewis

Chapter 16

Natalie folded her phone shut and sighed. "They have fixed the wheel on the lorry and are on the road again; should be here in about 4 hours, thank god."

Rob looked relived but when he spoke his voice was tinged with concern. "It still means the horses have been on the road for 20 hours. I hope Running Wind arrives fit. We only have 6 days to get him ready."

"I know, first that stupid strike delaying the aeroplane and now this. I wanted him here 2 or 3 days ago." Natalie was very worried about the extra stress her horse was under. The lorry had blown a tyre and lurched into the steel barrier. This would have unbalanced and severely disturbed all the horses. Running Wind was not a good traveller, something Natalie was always working on.

The riders crowded round the huge lorry ready to unload their precious equines. The atmosphere was tense. No one would be happy until they held their horse by his lead rein. One by one the exhausted beasts were slowly led out by the grooms on board. Running Wind, loaded first, was to be led out last by Rob, a special request which the transporters had reluctantly agreed to. Rob noticed that although most of the horses seemed un-affected by their long journey a few looked very shaky indeed. Each horse was quickly led off to be watered and fed, hosed down and groomed and finally allocated to their stable quarters for the duration of the games.

Natalie watched as Rob led her horse slowly down the ramp. As he walked off the ramp he stumbled slightly. To her dismay she could see he was trembling and shivering. The light rug he was wearing was rippling as if a sea of waves was passing beneath it.

"Rob look at him –what's wrong with him? "

"I don't know, but I saw three others doing the same."

"I'm going to get the vet, Rob. I'm not happy about this "

"OK. I will see to him and stable him."

By the time Natalie arrived with the vet Rob was very concerned about Running Wind. He had refused both food and water and was trembling even more. He looked lethargic and ill.

"Another one!" the vet sounded bemused as soon as he saw Running Wind. He confirmed that 3 other horses were showing the same symptoms. "I will take his blood too. I have asked the Olympic village lab to get me the results as soon as possible. I think it is shipping fever or pasturella. This infection is present in the mucous membranes and normally does not cause any trouble. However when a horse is stressed during transport and lacks food and water it manifests. We should have the results within a few hours." The vet quickly removed a syringe full of blood and left.

"A few hours, oh, Rob, how can I watch him suffer for so long he's so bad already." Suddenly Running Wind let out a huge bellow, sank to the straw and was trembling even more violently.

"We have to do something Rob- isn't there anything we can give him, is he missing something?"

Rob stopped short at this and without saying anything spun and ran off leaving a startled Natalie with her poor horse "Oh Toady! What's up with you boy?" Caressing her horses neck Natalie had tears glistening in her eyes. Running Wind shook again in long uncontrollable convulsions and Natalie instinctively held his head close to her breast. She wanted to will him better. Running Winds breathing was increasingly laboured, a yellow frothy discharge streaming from his nostrils. He was covered in sweat and his legs were paddling.

Rob was in his room in the Olympic village searching frantically, literally throwing his clothes and belongings around. This problem with the horses, it rang a bell. – God where was the damn book! He was sure he had brought it with him. Precious minutes were ticking away. He had to find the book. Finally, under the corner of his turned-down bed there it was –of course he had been reading it only last night finding the information and anecdotes fascinating. He thumbed so fast through the book he nearly missed what he was looking for. With relief at last he found it. A reference to a horse delayed on a journey whose symptoms were exactly those Running Wind was displaying. The horse was suffering from magnesium deficiency brought on by stress causing the release of adrenalin and other stress hormones which in their turn depleted the levels of magnesium and worsened the condition… Magnesium that's what he needed!! –where to get it though?

The veterinary block was only 5 minutes at a flat out run for Rob; at the door to the Lab a security guard blocked his way.

"Sorry, sir, only officials with special tags allowed in." The guard very gently pushed Rob back as he tried to rush into the clinic.

"It's very important I speak with the vet or one of the lab assistants."

"I am afraid it is absolutely forbidden for competitors or their team to enter this building. " The guard was insistent.

"May I speak with the vet out here then, please?" The desperation in Rob's voice touched the Guard, but he could not change the rules.

"Dr Santos is out seeing to a horse. I will ask him to see you when he returns."

Aware the clock was ticking and that he just had to get some magnesium as soon as possible Rob took off across the complex. Halfway to the entrance gate he came across one of the children belonging to the collective village workers riding on a small bicycle. Rob stopped and offered the child who was about ten $50 to borrow his bicycle.

"We have to ask my mother," the boy replied.

Rob sighed, more delay.

"Ask me what?" The voice came from just behind Rob. A tall lovely woman with smooth milk chocolate hued skin and an open friendly face towered over him.

Quickly he explained his request to the boy and the reason he wanted to borrow the bicycle.

"I have a better idea" The woman replied. "Quick come with me, I have a small motor scooter it will be faster than a bike or indeed a car as there is a lot of traffic on the roads. The closest chemist shop is 10 minutes away. Turn right out of the gate and left at the second set of traffic lights. It is the third shop on the left side.

They had reached the woman's apartment block and she pointed to a red motor scooter leaning on its stand.

Rob vaulted on the bike turned the keys and set off- a bit wobbly at first he set off so fast.

"Be careful." The woman called after him laughing.

Finally after an agonising half hour where Natalie saw Running Wind slowly growing worse she heard the loud tooting of a horn. She rushed out of the stable block. In the distance a red scooter was approaching at high speed. As it drew closer she saw it was Rob; clutched in his hand a small tube. He skidded to a halt and propped the bike up.

"Magnesium orotate tablets." He stated proudly to a very confused Natalie.

"What?"

"Don't question Nat we have no time to waste. Fetch me a little feed mash." Rob then took five of the 400mg tablets and crushed them in a container. Natalie ran back with the feed mash and Rob put a little into the container with the magnesium tablets which they took to Running Winds stable. The horse was really past wanting to eat but Rob desperately forced the feed into Running Wind who was too weak to put up much resistance and Rob was determined. Eventually the animal had swallowed most of it. They both watched astounded as only about 5 minutes after administrating the magnesium the terrible trembling stopped. A few minutes later and Running Wind clambered awkwardly to his feet.

"Rob, that was miraculous!" Natalie was deeply impressed. "How did you know what to do?"

"I'm pretty amazed myself how quick it was; just like in the book"

"Book?"

"Yeh I've been reading about horse nutrition and the importance of minerals. I found a great book recently by a woman who lives in Australia. Natural Horse Care by Pat Coleby. I have just read the chapter on minerals and she describes a case of travel tetany or magnesium deficiency. Stay here with the boy; I am going to offer some magnesium to the other riders whose horses are ill."

When Rob returned later he looked grim. "Two of the riders wanted to try the tablets and we had the same astonishing results. One rider refused insisting on waiting for the lab results. The horse was already down on its belly and I just heard it suffered cyanosis and died following severe convulsions."

Natalie flung her arms round Rob, "Oh, Rob, without your quick thinking Running Wind might be dead too. You are so wonderful."

Annika Warler knocked and entered the office of the Olympic Games equestrian director; Ramondo Setto looked up from his paperwork and sighed. Since she first arrived this Dutch woman had caused him nothing but grief. He just held back from saying, "What now!"

"Miss Warler, how can I help you?" Somehow he must force himself to be polite.

"I've come to complain about the behaviour of one of the other riders."

Tempted to say he did not imagine she had come to praise one, he simply gestured to the seat in front of him and said heavily. "I'm listening." He cocked his head and tried to look sympathetic and concerned, but this woman's demanding interfering ways were beginning to annoy him.

"It is one of the British riders.... a certain Natalie Diaz."

Now Annika had his interest. The beautiful graceful ex ballerina had stolen Ramondo's heart in her quiet elegant way. He had not missed the way she looked after her horse and only yesterday had been privileged to watch her practise some of her moves with her horse. After 30 years of being involved with

Olympic dressage riders he thought he would never see something so new, so original and so spiritually poignant. Watching Natalie perform with her horse had been a moment of sublime and inspirational gratification. His earlier annoyance resurfaced as he listened.

"Rules after all are there to be obeyed." she said petulantly. "Natalie actually works her horse in the arena with other horses--- with no head collar or bridle on."

Ramondo felt like saying *so what* but said instead. "I am sure Senorita Diaz has her horse under her control at all times and there is no risk to any other horse."

"There's no way she can be completely in control of her horse with no halter and lead rein or bridle. It's impossible."

Feeling as if he was being pushed into a corner by this obnoxious woman the director made a decision. "Do you know where senorita Diaz is right now?" He watched the jealous, childish face contort. "Yes. That's why I came. She is in the large practice arena with her horse free and I do not dare take my very valuable horse there –he is worth too much money. "

Ramondo did not miss that Annika did not say how upset she would be if anything happened to her horse –just out of pocket!

There were about eight horses in the arena when Ramondo and Annika approached. Natalie was in the far corner, a place unpopular with the other riders as it quickly became very muddy after the daily rain shower; no other rider was anywhere near her. The frightened whinny of a panicked horse met them, they ran -just in time to see a large chestnut gelding break free from its rider and take off trailing its rope. The poor traumatised horse sped round the arena its long lunge rope following behind in an extended snaking slither until it caught round the legs of another horse. The black mare reared and pulled back on her own lunge rope terrified of the sensation of the coil round her legs. Finally her handler had to let go and now two horses sped round. Hooves pounded as riders tried to steady their charges. The chestnut finally arrived in the far corner where Natalie was standing quietly with her un tethered horse. As the chestnut rushed past them, Natalie and her horse stood firm, the snaking rope suddenly lashed sideways and wrapped its coiling length round the legs of the stoical Running Wind. Although the horse took a couple of startled steps backwards he remained calm and seemed to be looking at Natalie to rescue him from the coil round his forelegs. Quietly, Natalie bent and unwound the rope. Meanwhile the black mare was nearly beside herself with panic. Screaming she ran round the arena completely out of control and managing to swipe several horses with the tail end of her lunge rope. Natalie calmly held the end of the chestnut's rope. Freed, it tried to set off once again. Standing tall she held firm to the end of the rope. When the dancing horse got to the end of the length it tensed, Natalie did not let go. She drifted with the horse bending and running a bit. Suddenly the horse halted for a few seconds to take stock of these new circumstances. As the horse stopped Natalie released the pressure quickly letting the rope slide between her hands. "Don't let go you fool!" Annika yelled. Ignoring not only the Dutch woman's words but also everyone else Natalie concentrated on the horse. It moved off again a few moments later with Natalie still holding the end of the rope as it sidestepped. Attempting to avoid the lunge line it barged straight into Running Wind who stood like a rock his eyes on Natalie. It seemed much quicker this time that the gelding halted. With lightning reflexes Natalie gave the horse immediate release. Swaying and blowing the chestnut looked at the rope then Natalie. Ramondo could see he was thinking of charging off again. Thankfully no one else moved and the black mare was at the other end of the arena. The chestnut horse finally gave a huge sigh and dropped his head. Natalie slowly gathered up the lunge rope and walked calmly towards the horse. His head high, he nevertheless let her approach and caress him. Jan Skaldic the horse's rider came over and performed an elegant bow to her as he took his horse from her. In the far corner the black mare was caught between two other riders.

"You see!" Annika spat at Ramondo. "Just what we do not need- horses careering free." The fact that the only horse not careering free had been Natalie's had obviously escaped this woman. Ramondo, however, did not know how to deal with this situation. It was obvious that not only was Natalie completely in control of her horse but also seemed more capable of controlling other people's too. But he had a responsibility to all the riders and if one horse was injured as a direct result of a decision of his he would pay and it would reflect badly on Rio and the games as a whole. Fortunately the grounds being used for the equestrian sports were very extensive Ramondo made an immediate decision. "We will create a further area for working horses a smaller private arena which can be booked by the hour and the competitors can work in this arena as they wish – either on a rope or at liberty if this is what the individual rider wants." The director looked straight at Natalie as he said this. Natalie rewarded him with a stunning smile making Ramondo regret too many rich meals and years having passed under his belt. Annika turned away from Ramondo at this, throwing him a sour look as she stalked off.

The director was true to his word and by early the next morning an oval pen had been created. Ramondo could not have told you why he had ordered this shape and not the round one suggested by his workforce, but oval it was. He had expected to see Natalie's name at the top of the list. To his amazement the first name was Annika's; with the next two hours booked by other members of the Dutch team. This meant that any rider coming after them would have to work in the heat of the day. Sure enough Natalie's name was fourth on the list; Ramondo swept back his copious steel grey hair and shook his head. That dreadful woman complained about Natalie working in the big arena and now she wanted to prevent Natalie using the space he had created to avoid this problem.

Deciding to go down and watch exactly why Senorita Warler needed a separate arena Ramondo walked across the compound. Halfway across he saw Natalie also heading to the new sand enclosure. Ramondo drew himself up to his full height which although not tall by European standards was easily 6 inches taller than the diminutive ballerina. He stepped alongside her with a very charming and graceful greeting and then they stopped and stood leaning on the wooden poles which made up the structure.

Annika had just led her horse into the arena. He was a very dark bay –not the coppery bright of Running Wind, but a handsome horse, however. Standing 17 hands high the Hanoverian was a powerhouse of muscle with a huge neck.

His eyes though were not soft and open, but glassy, and seemed to be looking inwards. As he stood by his rider's side he was quiet enough but his lips never stopped moving in a rubbery constant motion, almost as if he was talking to himself. When Annika mounted him, conversely, he manifested a different problem. He could not just stand still. His body was in constant motion along with his lips. He performed every move asked of him well enough but in a mechanical almost programmed way. Not only was there no expression in the work the horse actually looked depressed. *How much stress did it take for a horse to manifest such compulsive repetitive behaviour? Sometimes Ramondo had his doubts about certain dubious sides of the dressage world. On the bright side watching Natalie perform on her horse conveyed all that was the best in dressage. Her horse looked so willing and together with his rider his movements elegant and expressive like he was going forward into the bridle for comfort. Natalie would have been elated to hear Ramondo thought this, as this was ex-*

actly what Meredith had been looking for Natalie to find with her horse in her Level 4 work.

Ramondo not wishing to criticise any rider in front of another turned to Natalie his voice a little apologetic. "I'm sorry. Everyone else seems to now want to work in this arena, to be honest" His voice dropped to a whisper, "I intended this area for you to use."

"I know and believe me I am most grateful, but experience has taught me that callous jealousy is hard to deal with. You just have to live with it." Natalie smiled generously at Ramondo making his heart flip a beat. "Anyway we will have to perform in the heat of the day so I might as well get used to it."

Ramondo watched some of each of the riders in the new arena partly out of curiosity to see why they would need to be in a separate arena all of a sudden, but mostly so that when he watched Natalie it would not be especially remarked upon.

Although he had been checking his watch every few minutes Ramondo nearly missed Natalie working in the new oval pen. To say he was surprised by the beginning of Natalie's practice, would be a real understatement Natalie entered the arena with her horse then almost immediately released him. For a few minutes she just stood caressing the big gelding all over as he stood perfectly still a calm peaceful expression on his face. Natalie then picked up her whip, but this whip was unlike any Ramondo had ever seen before. The first part a non flexible dark green plastic attached to which fed through a leather loop was a 6' thin black string rope. Once when Natalie left her whip by mistake when called away to the phone Ramondo had picked it up to return it. He had been very impressed by the feel of it, not heavy and with great balance he had tried a few swings and found the rope expressive and easy to control. When he tapped himself on his shoulder with the stick part he felt nothing just a sensation like some one tapping you gently on the shoulder. It had none of the stinging lash of a schooling whip. Quietly

Ramondo watched as Natalie flicked the long string all over her horse with rhythmic stroking motions which reminded Ramondo of nothing so much as the tail of a mare gently fanning flies off her foal. When Natalie flicked the rope hard at the ground making a cracking sound then flicked the string all round Running Wind's legs, he did not move even a muscle. *No wonder this horse was the only one not to react to the rope round his legs, during the pandemonium yesterday. There is a lot to this woman's methods.* Ramondo was just imagining himself dining out with this exquisite woman and quizzing her about how she worked her horse when Rob Steel arrived. He placed a bag he was carrying on his shoulder next to the fence and waved at Natalie. Sighing Ramondo continued watching from his place on the fence.

As if she had been waiting for Rob to appear Natalie started to walk slowly round the arena. Her horse also walked exactly matching her pace. Running Wind was at her shoulder his ears expressive his eyes calm and trusting as he followed Natalie's cues. Ramondo saw that Rob had brought a small laptop computer with him which he had set up with a set of small speakers. Classical music drifted over and Ramondo tried to identify the composer. Natalie upped her pace to a slow run in perfect time with the music and her horse trotted next to her. When she changed direction so did the horse when she started skipping the horse was cantering. Suddenly she stood still and pointed to her left. Running Wind set off on a left circle round her after a few laps with the smallest of hand signals, so subtle Ramondo nearly missed it, Natalie asked the horse to return to her. This he immediately did, stopping right in front of her. She caressed his face then lifted her arm and asked him to set off to the right; again after a few laps she asked her horse to come to her this he willingly did and placed his head into Natalie's arms as she held him to her. Rob looked over and saw the expression on Ramondo's face he chuckled inwardly to himself *–If you liked*

196

this senor Romeo wait till you see the next bit! Although Rob was well aware of Ramondo's flirtatious attraction to Natalie; it did not bother him. Not only was he confident of Natalie's love for him but he welcomed Ramondo's efforts to protect the gentle Natalie from the vicious Dutch bitch.

Ramondo had successfully identified the music as being from *The Nutcracker Suite* by Tchaikovsky when the music changed tempo into the triangle peals of the *Fairy Dance*. Natalie her horseman's stick in her hand started to skip on the spot lifting her stick a little to the beat; Running Wind started performing a very beautiful piaffe beside her. As Natalie started to drift forwards slightly she remembered Tom's words, "Allow him to drift forwards a little to ease any tension. Then you can come back fresh next time. Do not press him too hard."

There's nothing you can't do, when the horse becomes a part of you.
Pat Parelli

Chapter 17

Three to go –oh God I just can't do this –so silly how many dressage competitions have we been through; to have such nerves now. But it is the most important one ever to ride for your country. Natalie looked down at her shaking hands. How was she going to get through this? Running Wind snorted his discomfort at Natalie's nerves. From his place on the special stands for the family and friends of the riders Rob saw with great concern the expression on Natalie's pale face. *Oh not now Natalie not in your special Kur performance no nerves. Just relax darling, oh how I wish I could will you courage!* She closed her eyes as the music for the next rider started up; the strains of the instruments came floating through the speakers just over her head. Her heart began to beat faster and lift. *Romeo and Juliet* she was swept back in time. All of a sudden she was 17 again, dancing in the end of term Gala with Shaun. As the music carried her along she danced again in her mind; cheek to cheek with her partner bending, stretching, rising and falling asif they were two parts of one being, that wonderful feeling of togetherness. Try though she might in all her career she had never danced like that with anyone else. She felt lifted, renewed, born again. That was it; of course! It was just like dancing in the woods. She and Running Wind would be like two parts of one whole. There was nothing they could not do.

The routines of the next two riders seemed to pass in a blur, but now Natalie was inpatient to perform --this was it! Like going on stage with Shaun. She was given the cue to advance and as she warmed up round the outside of the arena she felt Running Wind respond to her energy and confidence. Riding into the arena she just managed to flash a subdued grin at Rob. Startled Rob saw Natalie radiating confident energy with real pleasure in her eyes.

Running Wind had never looked so good, at his peak, he was now 13. His muscled neck was arched and his flanks gleaming, their copper tints flashing like a burnished pot in the bright sun. *Conquest of Paradise* by Vangelis boomed out of the speakers its dramatic beat seeming to throb through to the very cores of the spectators. Natalie entered the arena. She nodded to the judges and saluted then set off straight into a canter up to the far end where they performed a fantastic double canter pirouette with such expression the horse's left leg seemed to be rooted to the spot.The horse's ears were pricked and his tail swished almost in time with his legs. They then spun and cantered flat out to the other end where they performed another mirror image canter double pirouette. As they then set off across the arena in the extended trot; the horse was giving great reach on the corner at A. The music changed to another Vangelis composition the theme from *Chariots of Fire*, their transition to passage wonderful, the lift and elevation in front showing such height and freedom, this horse was giving the performance of his life. The crowd was completely silent. Running Wind, upbeat and flamboyant was following the music utterly in time and dancing with his whole heart. Rob observing was grinning like a Cheshire Cat. Ramondo knew he was watching the most moving and emotional performance he would probably ever see. Technically he knew the horse had made a couple of errors in the two time changes offering Natalie flying changes instead but if you counted the connection between horse and rider and the sheer quality of the dance Natalie should win gold, Ramondo knew in his heart, however, that the gold would go to the Dutchman on his black stallion. The music changed again to *Games Without Frontiers* by Peter Gabriel and Running Wind performed the most spectacular piaffe of his career his tapping hooves completely in time to the beat of the music.

Rob was unbelievably moved and thought sadly how much Bill would have loved to watch his boy at the Olympics.

Tom took Sue's hand in his as they sat together on their settee watching, Ellie curled at their feet had her new boxer puppy Mojo asleep in her lap. No one had spoken a word since Natalie's routine began. Sue realised that Natalie had taken dressage to music to a new level and the three just sat enchanted and watched. When Running Wind offered a fly change instead of the two times Sue knew the gold was lost, but what a brilliant performance!

Natalie had barely had time to recover from the emotions she felt at the end of her performance when the TV interviewer for the BBC appeared at her side.

"Miss Diaz may I congratulate you on behalf of the whole British Public for your marvellous contribution to these games , a team bronze and now this spectacular individual silver medal in the Kur"

Natalie stood holding her horse caressing his nose, he stood quietly beside her. The interviewer did not miss that Natalie had not handed her horse straight to a groom as all the other contestants had done. In fact, it was well known that she actually looked after her horse herself with help from her handsome boyfriend Rob Steel the jockey.

"Thank you," Natalie replied obviously nearly overcome with emotion, "But the real thanks must go to this marvellous boy here." she said kissing Running Wind on his nose." Without his supreme efforts and fantastic behaviour we could never have got so far. I owe a great debt also to Rob Steel and his sister Sue who with her husband Tom Mobley have been such a great and constant support to me and have taught me so much and polished our performance. I owe a special debt also to one man who sadly could not be here today as he is no longer with us; but whose memory and spirit live on in my heart- my dear Bill Harding."

Epilogue

She walks in beauty, like the night of endless charms and starry skies. And all that's best of dark and bright meet in her aspect and in her eyes.
Lord Byron

Last chapter

Natalie sat up in bed; a nightingale was singing its heart out in the oak tree outside the window. The cheerful warbling rising falling and changing every few notes did not for once cheer her. She knew she was being churlish and tried very hard not to be too annoyed with Rob. She looked at the clock 6.15. Rising she quickly washed and dressed, going downstairs she tried to re-member Rob's exact words to her last night. *Early start, long way, horse to fetch.* But what horse? There were no new horses to train coming in as far as she knew, and trust Rob to arrange such a thing on her birthday. Reminding herself she was not a child and had too much work to see to with Rob away she went outside. The green fresh feel of the April day, fields glistening in the dawn light as the grass was still wet with dew helped. By the time she had seen to all the horses and led Running Wind to his pasture she felt much better –just still a little peeved. She watched as her horse sauntered off down the paddock grazing a mouthful here and there making his way to the gap in the trees where he could look through and see the mares. Her love for her horse had deepened over the years and although he was 19 now and she had retired him from competing one of her favourite things was still a ride out in the countryside with him, usually helping Rob to take out a youngster. She wished they could ride out that day –well, maybe Rob would get back in time. Since they had bought the house and 20 acres there had not been much time to relax by themselves. Natalie had no regrets, though. Rob was still riding in the odd race but most of his time was taken up with training the 6 racehorses they had in the yard. Rob was a brilliant trainer who seemed to know instinctively when a young horse was ready. The wins had started coming and he was respected and popular. Natalie worked the youngsters with Quantum Savvy and Rob backed them. Natalie also now taught dressage and had a good schoolmaster in Roxy. When they bought the yard Sue and Ellie had given her the horse who was now 24 but still able to do a few lessons per week. "She has to earn her keep." Rob often joked. If Natalie missed anything she admitted to herself it was competing on Running Wind, but she did not want to press him. David had said his leg would be fine all his life but when he turned 19 she retired him.

The sound of the Range Rover and trailer bumping into the yard woke her out of her thoughts. Calling to Tim their lad to prepare the big stable she ran to meet Rob. The big stable was for the mares in foal planned for the future, but was the only one free at the moment as she also had two clients dressage horses at livery.

Natalie was amazed to see not just Rob's car but also Sue's, Melanie's and David's. She stopped short at this. Rob was just beginning to open the back door of the trailer.

"Here she is! "Ellie shouted.

Rob turned and flashed Natalie a huge grin. Everyone looked so happy.

"Would anyone like to fill **me** in with what's going on?" As she said it Natalie was aware she sounded a bit sharp.

"Oh, Natalie, don't be cross. Look!" As he said this Rob backed a horse from the box. Snorting the horse rushed out and spun round. Rob was, Natalie could see, struggling to control the horse. A load squeal rent the air and the horse danced sideways round Rob. Although the chestnut filly had been sweating in the box Natalie could see her quality and breeding. Her coat, gleaming gold and copper in the sun, she had a matching mane and tail; her left hind foot was white. Natalie was no expert, but she looked about a year old.

Motioning Natalie to approach Rob formally handed her the lead rope.

"Happy birthday, darling." He leant as if to kiss her and had to hurriedly side step out of the way as the filly swung her rear round. As Rob retreated laughing, Natalie shook the rope at the horse, gently at first then harder and harder until she took a step back. As soon as she took the step Natalie rewarded her with a release in the rope. She did this a few more times until the filly dropped her head and started licking and chewing. Natalie then stroked her head and mane.

This earned Natalie a round of applause from the gathered crowd of friends. Even Natalie was now laughing as she turned to Rob.

"She's beautiful, Rob, but how can you possibly afford to buy her?" At this Rob passed his wife the horse's papers." Look at her breeding."

Natalie quickly opened the passport and studied the horse's line. She did not read far before she stopped short gazing at the horse. Her Grandsire was Jet stream and she was out of Catcher in the Rye. Tears sprang into Natalie's eyes; she had the same Grandsire and Grand dam as Running Wind's Sire and Dam.

"From the same line as the boy!"–Natalie was clearly much moved. "But I still don't understand how we can afford her at all."

"Ah, well," Rob was still amused. "That's the catch with this present. The passport has shown you she has the same blood as Running Wind, -- well that's not all she has in common with him." He turned looking behind him and Melanie stepped forwards, "Actually she's even worse than he was." She, too, was laughing. "I had to work on her for two days to get her in the box. Her owner practically gave her away."

"We have Melanie to thank for her. "Rob put his arm round Melanie as he said this. "When she was contacted a couple of weeks ago about yet another difficult horse, she recognised the breeding from her papers and called me `I think I have found Natalie's new horse' was all she would tell me. I was as stunned as you when I found out. Her Dam is a top Trakehner."

Everyone turned then as Jeremy's Rolls drove into the yard. Jeremy, Kate and Claire got out of the car as the chauffeur went round to the boot and started setting up a small silver table on which he placed champagne flutes. He then took a magnum of Tattinger out, expertly opened it and poured. Handing round the glasses Jeremy raised his.

"To Natalie and her new horse--- Red Sun Storm!"

"Red Sun Storm!" The cry was taken up by Natalie's friends. Tears of pure joy were blurring her vision. Suddenly the filly obviously deciding she had stood still surrounded by all these people long enough, broke free tearing the rope from Natalie's hands and clattered up the cobbled yard. She was squealing as she ran. When she reached the stable doors she wheeled round and set off towards the paddocks. Her tail was high and she ran with exaggerated high floating movements.

The Healing Touch

Made in the USA
Charleston, SC
05 August 2011